The World's First Female Time Traveller

by

Dewi Heald

First published by Dream Jellyhouse in print on demand in 2021

Photography Copyright © Steve Scaddan 2021

Modelling by Elle Baldwinson

ISBN 978-1-7398579-0-5

Also by Dewi Heald :

Fiction

The Tale of Charlotte the Liberator

Cheese Market of the Future and Other Stories

Freaky Tuesday and Other Stories

~~Janet Chittock Likes Your Status~~

Me, I'm Like Legend, I Am

Land Of Song & Seaweed

Non-Fiction

The Seven Pillows of Wisdom

A Travelling Quaker Writes, Volume One

Music

Follow me on the Dai Bongos Channel on YouTube

All these titles are available through Amazon or from the author directly at dewiheald@gmail.com or currently through the website dewiheald.wixsite.com/rainbows

DEDICATION

Malo accepto stultus sapit

The World's First Female Time Traveller

Introduction

"Let me introduce myself," said the woman clicking her PowerPoint presentation forward to its first slide, "My name is Demerara-Lee Bowie and I was, I am and I will be, the world's first female time traveller."

There was a nervous rustling of papers among the delegates in the conference hall in front of her. Some people were checking how long this session lasted and whether it was then time for lunch.

"There is one question that I am sure that everyone asks time travellers who appear at scientific conferences," she continued, clicking forwards to another slide with five bullet points spaced equally down the screen, "will we ever get beyond PowerPoint? The answer is ... actually, you can't travel to the future because it doesn't exist, so we'll deal with that another time."

A ripple of laughter ran from the left of the hall, a ripple of confusion from the right of the hall and they met somewhere in the middle aisle with a group of people who were not listening in the first place, though they looked up to work out what the joke was. Luckily, the speaker was, is and will be used to this.

"Here are five things you need to know about me. At the age of five I was told by a hairdresser that I have an oddly-shaped head. I was named Demerara Bowie but I am not related to David Bowie. Bowie was not his surname anyway, whereas it is mine. I am also here at your conference to talk about my experiences of time travel.

You're going to be asking how I came to be known as Demerara. I was meant to be a boy and, in their disappointment, my parents refused to name me for several weeks. Finally, one day in a café they became so fed up with people asking if their baby had anything so dull as a name that my Dad was playing idly with a packet of sugar and saw the word 'demerara'.

If you want to use only half of my name, you can use 'Demi'. There's a science joke hidden in there. When I was growing up in Aberdare, they called me 'Demi-Lee' for short of course, but I have been Demi since I moved to Cardiff.

As for is it hard being a female time traveller as opposed to a male one then how about the fact that I have been talking for three minutes and all you have wanted to know about is my name? Kind of always feel like the time travel is a big deal too, but there we go. Yes, time travel is traditionally a male-dominated occupation, so I am something of an oddity."

Now the delegates were definitely shuffling in their seats, coughing nervously and not liking the confrontational edge that had come in to the proceedings. There were muttered comments that this woman was a definite 'oddity' and that in a line-up of presentations about serious matters of physics, she should not have been admitted. They liked to pretend that the scientific world had plenty of opportunities for women and well, if time travel was even possible, which everyone knows it is not, then surely women would do it too? A few delegates decided to write a list of female time travellers on their conference pack with their complimentary biro. There were a lot of blank lists.

Demi clicked on to another slide. This one had a picture of two teenage girls standing next to a jeep in a red desert and the words, 'How I Chose A Career In Time Travel'.

"Let me answer a few of your questions before you ask them," she said.

Part 1

I decided to become a time traveller at the age of ten. I knew that it was going to be hard as soon as I told Miss Phillips at school and she said 'oh dear, I'm afraid that girls don't become time travellers'. My school had only just caught on to the idea that girls might be interested in science and there were certainly no role models around for a girl who wanted to travel through time. You saw the abuse that Jodie Whittaker got when she became 'Doctor Who'? That's just a fictional role too, imagine the abuse waiting for a real life female time traveller.

I decided on this occupation when my best friend Georgina moved to Australia. Rather, her parents told my parents that they were going to move to Australia and my parents told me. I had the biggest fit that you could imagine. I was never a particularly loud or aggressive girl and yet I was no shrinking daffodil either. I had my happy little life at primary school in Aberdare and my small circle of friends, with Georgie at its centre. I had thought that going to big school in September was going to be my biggest challenge, but I was wrong.

Georgie and I were the traditional two peas from the same pod. As children we were often mistaken for sisters - both thin, pale and interesting though by the age of ten I had started to wear my dark hair longer and wanted a fringe to hide behind, whereas Georgie had started to want her hair cut short so her face could catch the sun.

We used to get up to great fun together. We used to wander off up the sides of the valley and fantasise about the dragons and the unicorns and the knights and the trolls that lived beyond in the Brecon Beacons.

Later I would find plenty of trolls across the mountain in Treorchy. Perhaps that reference is a bit local - it kills them at the Community Centre in Blaenllechau, mind.

That is one odd thing you know, the more you travel through both time and space, the more you want that sense of having roots somewhere, of having a spot that you can truly say is yours. Somewhere where your memories fall from the sky with the rain and are washed to the sea in the swollen rivers. That was Aberdare before Georgie left.

Our parents probably should have kept a better watch on us, but the long leash was a blessing as we would meet up in a ruined house on the hillside above the terrace where we lived and tell ghost stories. Our favourite was about the unemployed miner who fell on hard times and now haunted the abandoned house. We even put a sleeping bag and a pillow out for him and we swore that we went there once and it had been used.

Never for a moment did I doubt that Georgie and I would grow up together, go to big school together, fall in love with boys at the same time, marry at the same time (we would both be brides and chief bridesmaids on the same day), buy terraced houses next door to each other and be inseparable forever.

At no point in this plan did she move to the other side of the world. When I heard the news, I climbed the hillside to our abandoned house and screamed at the idea of losing her. I must have hurt my lungs doing it, the sound echoed and echoed and then died away to a broken-throated sob. Everything seemed to be unfair.

I tried to find out how much it would cost to go to Australia with her, but just before she was due to leave, I discovered that my junior saver bank account had lost a big chunk of the money I had saved! I told everyone that it was completely, totally and comprehensively unfair. You can tell from my language that teenage years were on the way.

I did the only logical thing in the situation. If I could not kick, scream and shout at Georgie's family until they reconsidered, I would have to travel back in time to stop their father being so stupidly selfish as to get a job in Perth. That was the day that I decided to become a time traveller. Who cared if it was an unsuitable job for a woman?

If this all seems a bit extreme, then remember that this was before you could make a free telephone call to Australia across the internet. Yes, there was e-mail but it was still slow and nothing like telling ghost stories with a torch late at night with my bestie. I knew that there would always be a Georgie-shaped empty space at the centre of my life that no-one else was the right shape for.

I was fortunate that Miss Phillips had felt worried about me and mentioned my unorthodox ambition to her boyfriend, a teacher in the big school in Pontypridd, Mr Johnson. Despite his average-sounding name, he was exotic to me as he came from London and his dark skin and deep voice made him an oddity in Aberdare.

My mother told me that it would be rude to ask him what he was doing in our area, so I never did. Besides, that was not important. What fascinated me was that he was a physics teacher. No longer was science going to be about trying to breed newts in the school pond, he was going to take me through the basics of the universe (while Dad sat in the next room pretending that he was not trying to listen in).

I will never forget the first time I asked him if time travel was possible. He replied, "Do you think that it is possible?" and I replied, "Yes". He told me that in science, anything was possible if you could prove it through experimentation. That was all I needed to know. I rejected coloured bracelets, dance crazes and the latest way to do your hair and dedicated the start of my teenage years to understanding science.

By the time I reached sixteen, I had hidden myself away with books and science and research for six years. I had grown that fringe as a first line of defence and was known as a geek in school. It did not matter as Mr Johnson had been impressed by my hunger for science and given me a succession of physics books, which I had eagerly devoured. My parents bought a toaster for his wedding to Miss Phillips and I invited them both to my sixteenth birthday party. They kindly declined, but you can see that people had forgotten that I was driven by loneliness and the need to make things right again.

I know that I should have been concentrating on puberty but that was like an annoying, buzzing fly banging on the window trying to get out. I was far too busy to open the window. My big surprise at sixteen was that my parents had saved up to buy me a plane ticket to Australia.

For my holiday reading, I bought a set of books about time travel. I worked on this theory that writings about time travel were actually accounts of it. If you could not publish your findings in a scientific journal, then maybe you would have them published another way? I tried a bit of H.G.Wells and then worked forwards. All these stories were about men, of course, but what if they were describing something actual?

Then when I arrived in Perth, I no longer had to make do with pictures attached to e-mails because standing on the other side of the arrivals gate was my best friend. We had such a big hug. Then her parents drove us through the night to their home.

It was my first experience of jet lag. Until then I had thought that the train to Pontypridd was draining, but this was something different. It was not the time difference, it was the feeling that my mind and body were in different places. I did not realise then that this was a hugely important preparation for travelling through time. No-one will mention it to you, but there is a form of jet lag from time travel too.

I am getting ahead of myself, mind. I was still only sixteen and stepping off the plane on a huge adventure. I am amazed my parents let me go, but I suppose that they were back home biting their fingernails while I was being whisked off from the airport past a hilariously-familiar sign saying 'Welshpool'. The Australian Welshpool was named after the wrong bit of Wales for me, but anything that reminded me of Wales was good.

I sat in the back of the car while Georgie's parents talked in the front. They were excited to be sharing their life, I think, but I looked out of the window and watched as we raced through Perth. I had not really thought about what Perth looked like or that it was just one bit of a massive continent - I was in Australia to see Georgie again and that was all that mattered.

I hardly remember that first night. I do remember that the temperature was nothing like I had imagined. Yes, I failed to appreciate that July was winter in Australia - I arrived in sun block and shorts and what I needed was a jumper.

I do remember Georgie looking so full of life. She was now tanned and athletic, whereas I was pale and a bit chubbier from all my studying indoors. It hardly matter and we chatted excitedly until the jet lag was too much and I fell fast asleep on a chair in the front room halfway through dinner.

The next morning ...okay, I was wide awake at two in the morning and then fast asleep at nine in the morning ... but I think that Georgie's family were used to visitors being like that for a few days. I was only just taking in that I was staying on a farm some way north of Perth itself.

Georgie was still little Georgie from Aberdare to me but I also realised that she had changed. Having dismissed my request to see Sydney Harbour Bridge with a laugh, she suggested we went out and about on the farm in a jeep. I grabbed the wide-brimmed leather hat that Dad had given me and said that I was ready.

Georgie also found my hat amusing, "Still got an oddly-shaped head then, Demi-Lee?"

"It's distinguished," I said, feeling the top of my head awkwardly.

"You're also dressed for the summer," she said, pointing to my shorts and light t-shirt.

"I am dressed for Australia," I said.

"It's ten degrees out there today," Georgie replied, "it's winter in WA."

I had no idea what 'WA' meant, but I knew that my knowledge was being questioned. I hated my knowledge being questioned, even by my bestie, so I shrugged and insisted that we set out. I had a hat to keep the sun off at any rate!

Georgie drove. I asked if that was legal and she just laughed and bounced about enthusiastically. What a sight we must have made! I held on to my hat as Georgie put her foot down. My hair blew in my face and I also tried to hold on to the jeep. This was very clearly out of my comfort zone!

The real difference with my best friend was that she talked like an Australian now too. Occasionally with me I heard her old accent creep through, but other than the odd 'cariad' thrown in or ending a sentence with 'see?', she sounded Australian. I was not expecting that. I sounded exactly the same as I had done six years before.

There we were speeding across the farm with Georgie laughing and pointing out all sorts of birds and trees that looked completely different to home. After a while the conversation dropped and the jeep just bounced along over the rough terrain. Then Georgie turned to me and with a sly smile that I did not recognise, asked me if I enjoyed the vibrations.

I was sixteen and embarrassed! I mean, of course, I could feel the jeep vibrating but ... well, I was embarrassed! That was the difference though, I was awkward and teenaged and wanting to ignore everything except my books on science but Georgie, she was now loving the outdoor life. We hit a particularly uneven patch of ground, the jeep bounced and my friend squealed with delight while I felt slightly sick. Make any comparison you like between the two of us, but now it felt as though we were peas from different pods.

This only made my desire to time travel grow stronger. You see, I did not resent this new Georgie, I loved her even more. I had once imagined that we would learn about boys and love and exams and growing up together, but now I knew that I needed this wild and crazy girl in my life to admire. She would tear down the main street in Aberdare in a jeep and drive everyone crazy! Perhaps that was a little extreme, but she would teach me how not to be shy and how to be free like her. I needed to find a way to stop her leaving. That day I decided to double my efforts.

*   *   *   *   *

I will tell you about the science at a later point. Let us just say for now that I returned from Australia and shoved my head into as many physics books as I could find. I must have had a kind of energy that only teenagers possess as I would study physics all day and in the evening meet up with Sam, Paula and Mary to buy cider in the supermarket and sit in the park all night. I gained some kind of popularity as I knew how to make fake IDs but that was a sideline compared to physics.

I exasperated my parents. Dad would buy me books about the history of Aberdare and tell me how his great uncle Len helped dig people out of the rubble in Aberfan, but I preferred physics. I think that when I gained a place at university in Cardiff, Mam and Dad were proud and relieved respectively.

What they did not know is that my research had led me to discover that there had been significant work done in the field of time travel in Cardiff University. I was thrilled to find this happening on my doorstep, though I wondered if it had been discounted by the scientific community precisely because it was not done at Oxford or Cambridge. Professors Leeds, Addicott and Braithwaite had written about the physics and I devoured everything that they had ever published on the subject. I was going to find my undergraduate studies pedestrian by comparison.

I took a job as an extra to help finance my studies. I had seen an advert in the local paper for women around the age of twenty to come forward for crowd scenes in a costume drama. Of course, I imagined flouncing around in a corset, but it turned out that they wanted peasants and I spent four days in mud. I loved it.

I loved it because I loved the research, see. On the first day, I was told in hair and make up that I had 'Victorian hair' and they needed to change it to 'Regency'. I was amazed to think that there was a difference and I studied the minutiae of fitting in to another age. Every time a job came up, I asked what age it was and then went away and immersed myself in what I could find about the culture of the time. I did not always get it right of course, I was turned down for a part set in Berlin in 1932, but the skill of fitting in was going to be a skill I would need for time travel.

I was either acting on an industrial estate in Wentloog or studying in the old Victorian physics building on Newport Road. I slept through my lectures and did the minimum for my seminars, but at some point in my undergraduate years in that old building with its carved statues of the past on its frontage, I discovered the way that I could restore my best friendship to what it should have been.

This is why I had my first conversation with Professor Leeds. Imagine a tall man with a small mop of white hair and one of those angular faces that made him look like a heron. I was all excitement about the idea, he was every inch caution and concern. Most importantly, he was the first person since Mr Johnson who accepted that when I discussed time travel, we were talking about something possible.

"Show me your workings," he said gruffly, as if I was still doing A-level Maths (double Maths in my case of course, passed with the highest mark that year).

I pulled out some papers and designs and started to explain that you can only travel in time and not in space, so you would go back to the same place.

"Not forwards to drive a hover car?" he enquired, with an arched white eyebrow.

"Impossible, the future doesn't exist yet and frankly, we're never getting hover cars," I said with a confidence borne of youthful ignorance of my limitations.

"Good girl!" he said, clapping his hands.

"Woman," I corrected him, "and so I need to construct a ..."

I stopped because he was shaking his head at me. He put a finger to his lips and took me through the network of corridors at the back of the departmental kitchen to what looked like a store room. This was the oldest part of the building, all high ceilings, cold walls and heavy doors. No-one ever came back here.

Leeds pushed open the door to the store room with some effort. Inside were piles of boxes, filing cabinets and there in the corner, what anyone who knew the physics would know was a time travel machine. Anyone who did not know the physics would probably mistake it for a shower cubicle ... with electronic controls inside. I must have gasped because Leeds grabbed my arm to stop me going forwards.

"Some rules," he said, "you can only go back to other versions of this store room. That means no earlier than 1871 ..."

"What?" I said, annoyed by him still having hold of my arm.

Leeds relaxed his grip and opened the top drawer of the filing cabinet next to the door. He leant against it and started to flick through a ream of papers with the university logo on them.

"Think about it Demi, you need the equipment ..." he was saying, but I was already at the machine, running my arm up and down its wooden frame and marvelling at the idea of how all my ideas about remaking my childhood could come true.

"Does anyone else ...?" I asked.

"There's a team at Trinity College, Dublin and another in Paris, but ... you need to take some time and do your research, you need to have some patience, I'll take you through the rules ..."

I thought through the rules - it was important that when I returned to the world where I was ten years old, I did not interact with anyone who might know me. It would weird people out.

My plan was simple, I remembered that there had been a delay between Georgie's Dad being offered the job and the family deciding to move. All I had to do was sneak into that gap, find a way to have the job offer withdrawn and then everyone would be happy. I could skip forward and see my friend as the Queen of Aberdare, taking everything in her stride and with me reflecting in her glory.

Professor Leeds was turning around with a folder from the filing cabinet saying, "You will need to fill in a few standard bits of paperwork before we can ..."

I was already gone.

Part 2

As I say, we will deal with the science another time, for now just accept that I travelled and found myself back in the world of my childhood.

My first reaction was a really bad stomach ache and a head that felt as though a hammer was being taken to it repeatedly. Oh yes, I am supposed to tell you about my amazement at how things had changed, about how quaint computers or phones used to be or something but no, I felt very sick indeed. I recognised this, of course, from my trip to Australia – it was like jet lag, only on a scale way beyond travelling in an aeroplane.

Later I would study 'time lag' a lot more carefully, but for now I just felt completely drained and as though my mind and body were in different places.

I managed to get back to Aberdare and hid out in the ruined house on the hillside where Georgie and I used to play. It was cold in there, but I found a moth-eaten sleeping bag and a pillow in a corner. I had not intended to stay long, but it would take time to recover from time lag and so a few days were needed. That was okay, I still remembered the PIN number for my junior saver bank account and I reckoned that I would be able to withdraw a chunk of money.

Those few cold, hungry days in the old house in the woods did wonders for my determination. I scoped out the layout of the factory where Georgie's Dad worked and then waited for my chance to sneak in and hide in the toilets when it came time for them to lock up for the night. There were no secure doors or laser sensors once you were inside the building and it was a short walk from the toilets to the main office. It was not a very secure effort, the filing cabinets in the Manager's office all had a key left in them at night and, while money was locked away, files were not.

Georgie's Dad had been one of only two candidates who they were considering for a job with their parent company down under, it seemed. The accomplished forger of teenage ID had no problems altering a few details in the files, making his qualifications less relevant, changing his experience and lowering the score on the interview scoring form for him. You would be surprised how straightforward it was.

On the day that ten year old me had thought of as the worst day of her life, twenty year old me went and hid behind the house and waited to see if the young me came tramping up with heavy footsteps, ready to hurt her lungs with screams so deep and loud that someone would assume animals were being slaughtered. She – or rather I – never arrived. I smiled. Georgie would be staying in Aberdare. I could go home, a process that would introduce me to 'time lag' on return journeys too.

*   *   *   *   *

I might have mastered – or possibly mistressed – the science of time travel, but I still lived with my parents. They assumed that I probably would do so until either my student life started to pay good money or until a man took me away from them. All they would know is that I had gone to university and returned that evening, not that I had spent three days in the past.

Professor Leeds was in the store room waiting for me of course, but I pushed past him and left him shouting for me to come back and fill in the paperwork. I headed straight back to Aberdare, full of excitement. It was as though I would be meeting a whole new person again – my best friend. What adventures we must have had, me and that crazy woman from the farm!

"Mam, Dad," I said rather breathlessly arriving home and trying to cope with that weird disconnect between head and body that time lag brings, "Thought I might go see Georgie."

"Sure Demi-Lee," said Mam, with a shrug of her shoulders, "you don't need to tell me when you're going next door."

Next door! This was it! She had not only stayed in Aberdare, she had moved in next door. Our terraced houses would lean against each other forever.

"Mind, you'll have nothing to talk to her about when the wedding's over, Demerara!" said Dad, without looking up.

The what? Whose wedding? I checked my hand and found no engagement ring, so I assumed not mine. Georgie was getting married, then? To whom? It had better be to a man who deserved her! No man was going to take her away from me, not after I had literally changed the world for her!

"Oh ssh you," said Mam to Dad, "you know that they'll be moving out after the wedding, let Demi-Lee enjoy her last days of living next door to Georgina."

"Leaving?" I asked and then, just to confuse my parents even more, added, "Number seventy-six or number seventy-two?"

I walked around to number seventy-six nervously. I had expected a different person, but not someone this different. Slowly the new memories that I had gained from being this person were coming to me – all the things that we had done between ten years old and now – but the sickness and the feeling of being lost and disoriented meant that I was struggling to work out which of them were from this timeline and which of them were from my original timeline.

"Demi-Lee!" shouted Georgie and gave me a big hug.

"I only live next door," I said with a sarcasm that felt like that was what I always said in response, "and I've told you it's Demi now."

"Oh shut up," she said playfully and hit me on the shoulder, "I'm glad you've popped over. There are centrepiece designs to look at."

"There are?"

Georgie was already in her house. She looked much the same as I had seen from her last photo from Australia back in my previous reality. Her brown hair was longer here, she had a fake tan rather than a farm tan and she wore jeans and a black top rather than outback gear, but it was still my best friend in them.

There was a shriek from inside and I hurried in to the front room to see her father bringing a jam jar down over a spider.

"Sorry, you know me and spiders!" Georgie said apologetically.

"But in Australia ..." I started.

"Still planning your big holiday?" asked Georgie's Dad convivially, "That's somewhere I've always wanted to go. You'll have to get a proper job to afford that, see."

"Derek!" said Georgie's Mam with a hard edge to her voice, "You know we're proud of Demi-Lee being the university one in the street."

Georgie's parents moved out of the way to let their daughter spread wedding magazines across the floor. I had the impression or the forming memory that this had been all they had done for the last three months. Why was there a slight feeling of disapproval coming through as well? Was she too young? Did they dislike her chosen man?

"Can't believe I'm losing you," I said.

Georgie looked at me and muttered something like 'you're not' before pointing at the designs that she had cut out and was now arranging on the floor.

"What do you do?" I asked, "I mean, humour me, what job?"

"What?" my bestie replied, "Sarah likes these ones by the way, but I'm not so sure. Are you okay? You look really pale. You know what I do. I work at that factory up the road and do the photography in my spare time. You're the brainy one – at least until tonight, you were!"

"You never drive a jeep?"

"Why would I want to do that?"

"For the vibration?"

"Sicko, what are you like? 'Spose you always were the adventurous one."

Now I wanted to march up the hillside and scream! Not this time for the loss of my friend but for the loss of the friend who I had known! This Georgie was lovely and happy and content but the wild spirit who I had met in Australia was just a regular woman in Aberdare now. How had I lived next to her and become the world's first female time traveller but she had become ...?

"I had an idea that all the guests could wear Tam O'Shanters," Georgie was saying excitedly.

"Tam o what?" I asked.

"You know, those Scottish caps that were suddenly all the rage. They said that they were worn by rebels against the annual St George's Day Parade in New York."

"I ... did I wear one?" I asked, a vague memory from this timeline starting to come into focus.

"What, despite your oddly-shaped head? Even you! Everyone did you idiot! You know the Americans and St George's Day!"

"They wear green and drink Guinness?"

"They wear pink and go pretend fox hunting on 5th Avenue! We drink gin and laugh at it every year – what is with you tonight?"

Georgie's parents must have given her a look that I was too tired to notice as Georgie corrected herself unconvincingly to "We drink orange juice, just orange juice."

I sat down heavily. This was not the world that I recognised and it was not the world that I had wanted to create. What on earth was going on?

"Perhaps you ought to ask one of the bridesmaids," I sighed.

"Them? Oh you know what's happened there, I've had to ask Hannah!"

Georgie's enthusiastic face dropped as she said the name and I tried very hard to remember who Hannah was and why I should disapprove of her. Have you ever fallen asleep in front of the TV while watching a film and then woken up half an hour later and not known the plot or the characters? That is what it felt like and I was desperate to know who this new antagonist was.

"Hannah?" I asked.

"No, not that Hannah, you know, Hannah Hannah."

"Hannah from Cwmbach?" I said, suddenly remembering a slightly annoying semi-friend who had wanted to get into painting and decorating.

"No!" said Georgie, looking appalled, "Not Darren's Hannah! I mean Hannah Hannah, the Hannah whose mother was seeing that man from Hirwaun behind her father's back and there was all that problem after he smashed the headlights on her car when he found out. You know ... Hannah!"

"Oh, that Hannah!" I said, lamely going for peace rather than comprehension.

"Well, I thought you'd be more upset about it, I have to say!" said Georgie, shuffling around on her knees among the magazines.

"What can I say? I've had a funny few days."

"You do look knackered, Demi-Lee," said Georgie's Dad and I nodded at him wearily, "that'll be because you're still young and able to get out and about and find out what you like, not try to make too many big decisions too soon."

I might have been suffering from a severe case of time lag and I might have been trying to cope with my best friend living in a terrace in Aberdare rather than a farm in Western Australia, but my goodness I recognised a parent making a dig at his daughter when I heard one.

Georgina pouted at her father as if she was still in her early teens and had only just discovered the art of slamming the door and yelling 'you've ruined my life!' He shrugged as if replying that he had made his views clear. I felt uncomfortable being used as an example of sanity in this situation. I did not even know who Hannah was, let alone Hannah Hannah.

Georgina very deliberately walked to the mantelpiece and picked up the picture of an attractive, blonde woman and said, "This is my favourite, of course," while hugging the picture to her chest and stroking her hand across the image of the woman's face.

"You were always a lesbian?" I asked, even more confused.

"Sleeping with girls will tend to do that to a woman," she said, with a chuckle to me but a sneer directed towards her father, "Demi, you really are in another time zone today. I'll always be thankful that you brought us together, though."

At this point, Georgie's parents both shuffled awkwardly and made excuses to go into the kitchen. If they were trying to hide their disapproval of their daughter marrying a woman, they were as good at it as their daughter was at trying to hide her liking for gin.

We sat there on opposite sofa seats for a few moments, me tired of travel, my friend tired of her parents. My thoughts were still jumbled all over the place and I found myself pondering my past out loud.

"It was because he was black, wasn't it? Mr Johnson - you remember, the guy who got me turned on to physics - I never really said it out loud, that's why people were suspicious."

Georgie stood up and put Sarah's photo back on the mantelpiece as carefully as if she were placing a blanket over the real woman while she was sleeping. Then she walked over and gave me a hug, an awkward operation as I stayed sitting in the chair while she did it.

"Oh Demi, we turned out so different, but I am so glad that we said that we would always be friends."

"Do you ever think about ... I don't know how to explain this ... do you ... I don't know .. think what if your Dad had got that job in Australia?"

Georgie stared at me. It was as if she was the one with the time lag for a minute and was trying to remember an event that had some emotional resonance for her, but not enough to make an easily-accessed memory.

"Ages ago? When we were children? No way, I'm glad that never happened. I'd have missed you. How would I have coped with the spiders? And all that space? No, home girl me. Sarah's my soulmate. We're going to find a place to live, see if we can have children. All respect Chief Bridesmaid, you look so tired, we ought to do this another time. Centrepieces can wait."

That night I was sitting in the ruined house, long after my parents had gone to bed, thinking that time travel is the worst job in the world.

You have probably seen one of those Richard Curtis films, "About Time" where the male lead tries to solve all the problems in the female characters' lives? As if they couldn't do it themselves. Sorry, personal bugbear of mine, bad time travel films ... not to mention bad romantic comedies. Anyway, imagine if that was your dilemma.

You could solve all the problems in someone's life, but they would change as a person. Really all those women in that film who have problem-free lives due to the time traveller should end up arrogant, conceited and with no resilience. Without hardship, you do not grow. So, you want your friends to grow but you also do not want them to suffer. Yet, you cannot have both and you have the power to change one or the other. Which

23

do you choose? Do you make your friends suffer or do you stop their growth?

This is one reason why you have never met a time traveller. You know that you would ask them to change something in your life. Yet, all those things that you would gladly change have made you who you are now.

It was 3 a.m. in the morning and I was wide awake and cold. At that point, I never wanted to travel through time again.

Part 3

Demi paused to take a drink from her glass of water. Her audience still looked sceptical, but some of them were at least listening. She had deliberately dressed up to look smart and professional. Her shoes were killing her – ha, there was a recommendation, she thought, time travellers should wear comfortable shoes.

In the pause, a number of hands were raised. She had said that there were no stupid questions and so long as this was not another one asking what the capital of Kenya is, then she would be fine. Actually, she once tried to change the capital of Kenya just to stop that question, but that was another story, a story in which a white woman with a blonde streak through her dark hair really does not help the cause of Kenyan independence.

"I believe all this," said a middle-aged man with serious glasses who clearly did not believe a word of what she was saying, "but are you saying that your time travel turned your friend into a lesbian?"

"No," replied Demi, mentally reviewing the idea that there were no stupid questions, "I think that Georgie was born a girl who liked girls and that to my surprise she explored that in her Aberdare life earlier than in the ... OTL. That's 'Original Time Line', which is how time travellers refer to things before we mess with them."

There was a mumbling along the front row and the man who had asked the question did not seem to be satisfied with the answer. A younger, smarter man sitting next to him, who looked less convinced that she was talking sense, now raised his hand and spoke before Demi nodded to take his question.

"I work in academia though - where's the oversight? Who funds you? How could you ever get away with this without proper scrutiny?"

Demi pressed a button on a small pad in front of her and the presentation moved to the next picture. The title said, "Time Travel - the Early Years". It was an ambiguous title that she had liked ... clearly more than her audience did.

*   *   *   *   *

I have no idea if Georgie was happier in Aberdare than in Western Australia. The truth is that I would never know. I realised that we made these decisions all the time, always telling ourselves that we were doing something because it would be better for someone else. For a non-time traveller (a 'stationary' as you are called), the great gift is that you never get to see what Aunt Beryl's life would have been like had she not been put in a care home. You can always kid yourself that you made the right decision because you never see the evidence to compare the two situations. Believe me, that really is the better way to live.

However, I did know that Professor Leeds wanted to see me in his office as soon as I stepped back on university property and that I was in major trouble. I was still only twenty at this point, so I decided to confront the situation with the only two strong suits that twenty year olds have - high spirits and silliness.

Professor Leeds's office was filled with pictures, many more than you would normally see in an office, mostly framed photographs taken from different times. I was curious enough to turn around the one on his desk that was facing away from me - it was a framed bus ticket and a picture of a suburban house with the words 'Saturday October 25th 1965, King's College' written on it.

"Is that somewhere you've been?" I asked rather stupidly.

"It may be somewhere you've been if you can take this seriously," he replied.

"Look, it's cool," I said as if he had been the one to do something wrong, "I got back okay."

"Except it's not cool," he replied, "you cannot go running off without telling me where and when. You can kill yourself time travelling. We lost Dr Braithwaite because he tried to go back before 1871."

"What's the point of 1871?" I asked, playing with the stapler on his desk.

"It's when the storeroom was built - you can only go back to a point where it exists. Braithwaite tried to get back before that and we think he died in a political protest in 1848. Messy stuff. You have to be aware of what you are playing with."

I gave a sudden yelp as I accidentally closed the stapler over my finger. The staple drew a small prick of blood and I placed the stapler back on the desk. I sucked on my bloodied finger and felt foolish.

"I'm willing to teach you what I know, but you have to take it seriously."

"Sure," I said, trying to add a tiny amount of gravitas to my voice.

Leeds stood up and looked out of the window at the back of his office. You could not see much beyond an empty car park where there was building work going on, but he seemed to ponder it for a long time.

"I have an offer to make you. I will ask the university to give you a credit for a module called something like Chronological Studies and if you can follow what I teach you, then I will sign it off. You can always do it instead of Dr Hammacott's lectures."

"That's okay," I said happily, "I've been skipping Dr Hammacott's lectures."

"I know," he replied sternly, waiting for my face to fall before adding, "you are the most talented of the potential time travellers I have met here, but you need to pass your degree and you need to learn the rules."

"Rules are for ..." I started and then stopped as I realised that this man was offering me the chance to study my obsession of the last ten years. I also realised that not passing my degree was going to cause some problems for my ambition to study further. Once you have travelled in time, it is quite hard to keep perspective.

"Once a week, in my office, same time as Hammacott's lectures. No travelling without permission. Every trip has to be signed off by me – no questions."

"Not even 'what's the capital of Kenya?'" I hazarded.

"There are stupid questions, just remember that."

I nodded and felt glad that he had not questioned me about how I had messed up Georgie's life.

*　*　*　*　*

The first lesson was called 'research'. I sat in the office with my notepad balanced on my lap, scrawling away notes as Professor Leeds spoke. He turned out to be more engaging than I had imagined. If he had been in his twenties in the 1960s, I reckoned on him being in his seventies now, but there was something about him that sparkled when he talked about time travel. He was stern about the rules though. You had to research where you were going and you had to avoid intervention. Here was his example -

"Did you read the book 'The Time Traveller's Wife'?" he asked.

"Yes - I have always had this theory that time travel books are written by real time travellers because they can't get published as research," I replied, jabbing my pen into the page as if to re-enforce the point.

"Spot on, my girl!" he said with a smile.

"Woman," I corrected him again.

"Okay, okay. I remember reading reviews of the book when it came out. People criticised the main character – the time traveller who is ..."

"Male?"

"Yes, but ... well, I suppose that there haven't been many female time travellers other than ... who was the main character in 'A Wrinkle In Time'?"

"Never heard of it."

Leeds walked over to his bookshelf and looked at it, though I was sure that it was only physics books in front of him. He did not look at me when he spoke, though he tucked his hands into his trouser pockets in a way that did not seem to fit his age or demeanour.

"It was big in the sixties - American book - I have it somewhere at home. Written by a woman writer."

"Or a writer as we would call her now," I took pleasure in correcting him.

Leeds turned back to face me and he had a slim book in his hand. He threw it on to his desk and it skidded towards me until it hit the photo frame. I looked at it and it was a copy of 'The Time Machine' by H.G. Wells with an illustration on the cover that looked like it came from a pre-moon landing vision of a future in space.

Leeds nodded towards it and so I leaned forward and picked it up. It was old and a couple of the browned pages were loose and needed to be kept in place as I flicked through it.

"1964," I said, confirming my belief that this edition was published before the moon landing changed perceptions of future fiction, but also wanting to tease him a little, "that's ancient."

Leeds sat behind his desk and looked like he did not know if he wanted to admonish me, sigh or just tell me that he was annoyed, "Demerara, I know that you are teasing me, but I am here as a mentor, not a friend. I know that you are only young, but time travel is a serious business."

"Look," I said, waving the aging book at him, "I tried reading this when I first studied the subject. It starts with this bloke lecturing people about his discoveries. I wouldn't do that and anyway, it's about the future. You can't travel to the future, we know that!"

I hoped that the use of 'we' would convince him that I was feeling fully part of the time travel community.

"Part of your homework for this week is to read it and see what you can learn. There are other books about it, some have female heroes - heroines? Heroes? You tell me the grammar. There was one a few years ago, title was something about a dog, Addicot gave it to me. Bit of a joke in time-travelling circles to give each other novels about time travel."

"Bet you're all just a hoot at parties," I muttered grumpily.

I tried my best smile and pointed down to my notepad in the hope that he would go back to the lecture and stop criticising me.

"Okay, back to what literature can tell us," he said, "The reviews of 'The Time Traveller's Wife' criticised the time traveller for knowing that the September 11th attacks on the USA were going to happen but not trying to stop them. Those people would be the same ones who think that time travellers spend their days trying to alter history."

I was still surprised to hear the word 'traveller' in the plural. I had thought that maybe it was just the elderly professors here and me, the world's first ... oh, I could look that other stuff up another time.

Leeds was still speaking, "The USA knew about the September 11th attacks – Ahmad Shah Massoud addressed the European parliament in early 2001 and said that he had credible evidence that a Saudi group were already well underway with a major attack on the USA. The warnings were ignored. Those were warnings from a man on the ground in Afghanistan who knew terrorist networks. If they did not believe him, why would they believe a man turning up saying that he is a time traveller and has seen the future? What chance would a woman have?"

I sat back and looked at him carefully. He was studying me for a reaction and I realised that my initial time travel journeys had all been about changing the world for me. I had been shamefully unaware of the idea of changing the world for others. Yet he was telling me not to try to do it.

"Then you are dealing with all the variables and all the people involved in a major incident like those attacks. It is just far too much for one person to alter. If we could ever get together a group of time travellers to work together ... but co-operation is almost nil. Well, it was until Brexit and you have two different groups of travellers fighting over that ... but I keep out of that and ... just keep out of that please, Demi."

This was all the most amazing detail to me. I had sketched a plan, but he was colouring it in with every sentence. He impressed on me the need to research and showed me a twenty pound note to make his point. This design of the note had not even been legal tender a few years ago and people underestimated all those subtle changes that will make you stand out. Having raided the junior bank account owned by my younger self once already in this timeline, I took his point.

"I get all this from being an extra," I explained, "there's an audition next week for a BBC Wales musical production based on the life of Laszlo Biro. It's to mark a Wales-Hungary historical project or something. Anyway, I have started to research Hungary in the 1930s."

Leeds could tell when I was bluffing, something that I found hard to understand at first.

"What research have you done so far?" he asked.

"I've ordered goulash in the university canteen," I offered before holding up my pen hopefully and adding, "I'm also well-acquainted with his invention."

Leeds shook his head and strode back to the window. I could see that he was exasperated with me and worried that I would be putting myself in danger without adequate research. I wanted urgently to change the subject.

"Isn't there something that you would want to change?" I asked, folding my notebook shut as my sign that I thought that our first session was at an end.

"The treachery of the blue books," he replied and then his shoulders slumped and he sighed at the lack of comprehension on my face, "don't they teach you any Welsh history?"

I put a hand up to tell him to pause and took my phone out with the other hand and started pressing the screen.

"Oh for crying out loud! History is for the classroom, not the internet! We can't rely on a generation of ..."

"Ssh! I'm reading," I replied.

He stood there with the closest thing to a pout that he could manage while I scanned the entry on Wikipedia. To be honest, it was partly out of some misguided youthful idea of 'taking control of the situation'. When I had finished reading, I lowered my hand, put the phone away and smiled at him.

"OMG! They said that the Welsh were immoral, ignorant and lazy! Well, Jenny Jones and Rhiannon Fisher I grant you, but not everyone!"

"You're not taking this seriously ..."

"Treachery of the blue books," I said, "got it. You see, that's all you need anywhere you go."

"And what do you think that the wifi would have been like in Aberdare in 1885?" he asked.

"Could be about the same as it is now!" I said with a laugh and then, when I noticed the seriousness of his look, simply added, "'Point."

Leeds moved round to my side of his desk and sat down on it, carefully brushing the stapler to one side.

"Things have changed is what I am trying to say and you need to be careful."

The light coming through the window was catching the side of his face. Maybe the sun was hiding behind a cloud or a tree but suddenly the office seemed darker and the Professor seemed older. I felt guilty for my light-hearted exuberance.

"Sorry," I said, "I get it and, you know, I wish that I spoke Welsh when I read things like that."

"You should do," Leeds said with a sigh and then fixed me with his serious look and asked, "Do you promise me that you will not try to stop 9/11?"

"I will not try to stop 9/11," I replied truthfully.

Of course I was not going to stop 9/11. I am a valleys girl. I was going to stop Aberfan.

* * * * *

There is a time travellers' joke that goes something like this. The great time traveller returns to the present after the historic mission. He (of course) steps back out into the university research department and announces grandly, "I did it! I killed Hitler!" He is expecting accolades from all his fellow scientists, but they simply look at him and ask, "Who's Hitler?"

If I told you that once upon a time a coal tip slid off a mountainside and destroyed a school and houses in the town below, then I reckon that if you had never heard of it before, then you would think that I was making it up.

We never learned about it properly at school. I remember one of the teachers who was a vicar talking about passing a roadsign for Aberfan and wanting to cry, yet I also remember not being able to comprehend 116 children and 28 adults dying. It was only as I became a teenager that I realised how horrific that was. I still think that plenty of people outside Wales have never stopped to contemplate it. Of course I would want to stop it.

I knew that I would not have permission to do it from Professor Leeds and so I worked away in secret. I bought some clothes in a vintage shop and I went to a set designer at the extras company and asked if I could borrow some things for a drama set in 1966. She seemed convinced and even gave me tips on hairstyle and make-up.

I was ready except, of course, I was not in the least bit ready. Firstly, there was the awful time lag when I arrived back in 1966. I felt nauseous and weak, as if my head and body had once again found their way to different time zones. In my youthful feeling of invincibility, I had only allowed myself two days to go to Aberfan, warn people about what was going to happen and then return to Cardiff before the tragedy was due. My assumption was that there would be some kind of evacuation of the area, people would be taken to safety and an extraordinary disaster would be averted. I had not been listening to my first lesson carefully enough.

I made it to Aberfan, despite the time travel sickness, but it was a different place to the one that I had known. It is hard to explain, but history to me had been a school trip to Big Pit to see something that was once a coal mine or to the Rhondda Heritage Park to see ... something that was once a coal mine.

Everywhere you went in the valleys, the tourist infrastructure told you that you were living somewhere that was once interesting. Shame about the present or the future, but outsiders would pay to look at your past.

If you want to be technical, coal-mining was already in decline by 1966, but it still dominated the area where I would later grow up. Now I realised that when Georgie and I had gone and walked in open, green fields or on hillsides with new flowers coming through the ground, these were old collieries. Of course our ghost stories had included tales of men trapped in mine shafts and the dog that led its owners into an abandoned mine where they found a horde of diamonds and so on ... but this was real. Yes, it had all the ugliness of heavy industry, but it also defined the place. I grew up in a place that people talked about leaving. Back in 1966, I realised that it must have been an area where people stayed.

It rained too, of course. I had brought a coat which had been fashionable in a time when the outdoor adventurer look was in. I had not remembered how much it would make me stand out. I started out trying to play up my Aberdare accent and soon fell back to something that might excuse me.

"I'm Cecilia Hardcastle from London," I would say to people with an exaggerated English accent and an outstretched hand, "I need to talk to you about the mining here."

Oh goodness me, it is embarrassing to recall. I was naïve enough to believe that all I had to do was to tell people to clear the school and to have the tip investigated and they would listen, but they did not listen. Some nodded their heads, some said that they had wondered the same thing for years, others told me to write to the National Coal Board, but no-one wanted to do anything and my increasing sense of urgency only made them think that I was even weirder.

By the end of the first day I was in tears and I had to return. I could not stay there and witness the tragedy itself.

Back in the present day, I decided to pause and regroup. What I really needed was to be further upstream so to speak, and to find someone who would listen to me and a reason for them to listen to me.

Meanwhile, I still had my weekly Chronological Studies session and the next Tuesday Professor Leeds found me hiding out on the second floor of the university library, head buried in a large book. Luckily, I had thought ahead.

Leeds sat on the side of the table and I pretended not to notice him at first. He tapped his fingers on the table impatiently and the students next to me stood up and moved away, fearing something was about to happen.

"You thinking of popping in today, Demerara?" he asked.

"Oh yes, is it that time? I was just reading this fascinating book!" I said, hoping my strong suit could also be youthful innocence.

Leeds leaned over and took the book from my hands. The front cover picture was of a group of Victorian women at a concert.

"A History of Aberdare?" he read from the cover and then flipped to the inside page where there was a blue biro scrawl, "'To my daughter to celebrate going to university and in the hope that she finds a proper subject to study. Love Dad.' Supportive of your life in physics, I see."

"I have my challenges," I said, taking the book back.

"Well, it's good to see you taking your research seriously. Perhaps we can discuss a trip to Aberdare in 1885 if that's your interest. A field trip to look at ..."

"I'm in," I said, stuffing the book into my backpack. The joke was on Leeds though. Hidden in the centre pages of the book was a document on mining technology that I had slipped in there while in the university archives earlier that day.

I am sure that I am not the first woman to hide geological data in a history of Aberdare, but Dad's book had come in handy at last.

Of course, I was too young to really think about all this from anyone else's point of view. I should say that before Leeds retired, I was lucky enough to have the chance to ask him what it was like when I headed off to Aberdare in 1885 following our conversation that day, some research and a fitting for Victorian corsetry. He told me that I had been 'impossible', followed by 'annoying' and then 'irritating'. I asked him why he did not intervene or try to make me behave more responsibly and he simply shrugged his shoulders and said that he knew that I had to make my own mistakes and that that had been a lesson for him to learn.

"They found a hat for your oddly-shaped head, I see," was his only observation before I left.

For me it was a week in 1885, for him it was an hour of nerves and not sitting still. Still, I did come back in one piece and stepped out of the cubicle looking a little more tired and a lot more disgruntled than I had been when I left.

"Well?," he said with a smile.

"You knew, didn't you?" I said accusingly, carefully pulling at a piece of my Victorian dress which had become trapped in the cubicle door.

"I did try to tell you," he replied.

"Did it change so quickly?" I asked, as we were walking down the corridor to his office, "I mean, from everyone speaking Welsh?"

"The Treachery of the Blue Books," he repeated, "they had tried to suppress the Welsh language for centuries but it was attacking education that really did it. But that's not this week's lesson."

I sighed and slumped down in a modern seat as best as a Victorian corset would allow me. There was something more than language I wanted to talk about, but I was struggling for the words.

"It was the feel of the town that got me."

Leeds looked for a glass of water, even though a whisky would have done me more good.

I continued, "Did you know it was a centre of music and publishing? When did it all change? When did we stop caring about places and the people who live in them?"

Leeds handed me the glass of water and I gulped it greedily. I could feel that the time lag from this trip was going to be tough and I was babbling.

"The lesson is that sometimes you can fit in better by being an obvious outsider. People will find differences less remarkable if they are expecting them and ..."

"I'm serious," I said, ignoring the lesson that I should have been learning, "When did some towns just become wreckage in society's changes?"

Leeds shrugged and sat back on his desk, "Why do some people's lives not matter as much as other people's? Why is it okay for some people to live in danger when others are protected? Have you ever studied the Aberfan disaster?"

I coughed and muttered something vague into the glass of water.

*　*　*　*　*

Yet I had learned a lesson. I needed to become the knowledgeable and convincing outsider. My skills at forging ID documents came in handy as I transformed myself into Cecilia Hardcastle, Mine Engineering Expert with a string of technical qualifications from King's College, London and an obscure mining institute in Cornwall. I comforted myself with the idea that if I failed my degree, I could probably still forge a certificate for it.

Oh, I had studied. I could tell you everything that you wanted to know about colliery spoil tips, underwater springs and the danger of slurry. By the time I was standing in front of Merthyr Tydfil Council in July 1963, I spoke with the authority that comes from a forged ID card but also the passion of someone who needed to avert a disaster. They listened, they questioned and then they re-assured me that I could return to London safe in the knowledge that they would be taking this up with the National Coal Board over the subsequent year.

A year was fine, it was another three years until the tragedy would happen. I had done it! I could return home with the feeling of having done something good with my talent for physics at last.

Back in the store room in the present, Professor Leeds was waiting for me. He shook his head as I stepped out of the cubicle.

"You just don't understand it, do you?" he said, "I know when you travel - the university experiences a power surge, it's obvious. You've done it twice now!"

"I have averted tragedy. You should be praising me," I announced grandly.

"If it's 9/11, Miss Messiah, then you failed on that one," he said, walking away from me.

"It's Ms Messiah," I shouted after him, while I tried to find where I had left my mobile phone. I found the phone and ran down the corridor behind him, tapping the screen as I did.

"Look! Look! I'll tap something into Wikipedia and it won't bring up any results, you won't believe what I've done!" I yelled after him.

My mentor continued to walk away from me. A few seconds later, there were a lot of loud, repeated unladylike words as I read the Wikipedia entry about the Aberfan disaster. Under 'Background' it noted that the local Council made repeated warnings to the National Coal Board after July 1963 but that they were never listened to.

My f-words delivered at full voice, I slumped down to the floor in the corridor. What the hell did I have to do? I failed Georgie and now I was failing to even make a difference to the world. Was I the world's worst time traveller? What on earth was it all for?

As I sat on the floor and cried, the contents of my handbag rolled out across the cold tiles. A deodorant can rolled into my leg and bounced off, but I did not care.

Then I noticed a card that had not been there before I travelled. It was the size of a business card, but looked as though it had been tucked into the top of the handbag by someone as I passed them.

Along with a strange green and red logo that looked like a speech bubble, it had the words –

Time Travellers Anonymous (TTA)

Meetings : Berlin, every November 1932

There were others. I wanted to meet them.

Part 4

There was an arm raised in the third row of the audience. It belonged to a middle-aged man with a bow tie and glasses. Demi was prepared to explain her research into mine workings or her impressions of the National Eisteddfod of 1885 and nodded for the man to ask his question.

"Surely though if your friend's memories changed so that she never remembered going to Australia, so your memories would change so you didn't remember it either?" he said with a smug and satisfied smile on his face.

Demi took another sip from her water glass and then put it back down on the table next to her. Ah well, at least it was not a question about the capital of Kenya. She shook her head at the man.

"No, this is another reason why time travel is a harder job than films ever tell you. You here all have the memories from the OTL - original time line - only, but I have several different sets. I remember drinking cider in the park with Georgie, Sam, Paula and Mary. However, in the time line we live in now, Mary wasn't there. So, I often get mistaken about who did what and when. Yeah, you get time lag, but you also get this extraordinary pressure of having contradictory memories. I would not recommend that my daughter went into time travel, put it that way."

"I don't remember that craze for Tam O'Shanters that you mentioned ..." the questioner started, but Demi had had enough of stupid questions.

She pressed a button on the small pad in front of her and the presentation moved on to the next picture. This showed a picture of a big mug of steaming coffee and the title, "Time Travel Addiction."

* * * * *

Nail-biters will know what I mean. Anyone who has ever picked a scab, scratched their eczema or pulled at a plaster will know what I mean. You know that it is not good for you, but you feel this compulsion to do it. I may have made fake ID and drunk cheap cider in a park as a teenager, but I was remarkably free of other vices. I knew, however, that time travel was addictive.

The Time Travellers Anonymous card stayed tucked into an inside pocket in my purse, accidentally glued between my student union card and a money off card for Coffee Nirvana. I told myself both that I did not need the card and yet I also did not throw it away.

Georgie and Sarah had a beautiful wedding, I passed my Chronological Studies module and my degree soon followed. Mam and Dad looked so pleased at my graduation that I could never bring myself to tell them that I had only passed thanks to my unorthodox tutelage from Professor Leeds. I told Mam that I was sad not to have gained a First, but she remarked, "only person I ever met who has a First Class degree is Hannah Thompson's father and that's only because he got it in prison."

I started to tell myself that I did not need time travel in my life and that the desire to meet other time travellers was a passing phase. I joined a gym and finally started to try to look a bit more like a young woman who spends a little time outdoors occassionally.

Naturally I enrolled in a Masters degree, despite Dad asking when I would 'get a proper job'. Occasionally, I would have a few too many drinks and tell someone that I was a time traveller. I used to attract sci-fi nerds and geeks and they would love that. I think that I ended up getting far too friendly with a

42

couple of them because they thought that a woman pretending to be from another time was a turn-on.

No-one ever believed that I had travelled in time of course and often those who challenged me would ask, "Why don't you kill Hitler?" My standard answer would be, "He's alive in this time line, is he? Dammit, that suitcase didn't explode at the right moment, then?"

I was not time travelling, but still the itch felt like it needed to be scratched. I had the odd temptation when two social events clashed, to go to one and then go back and enjoy the other one too or to be prepared with champagne plus strawberries and cream ready by the side of the bed when I met a man on a night out, but otherwise I was happy being 'stationary'.

I dedicated myself to studying the theoretical side of time travel rather than the practical application. Time lag was an interesting subject, as was trying to understand what happened if you travelled back to before 1871. Aberfan had taught me that there was no point trying to interfere in history and so I did not see the point of it ... mostly.

However, you know that the itch does not go away just because you do not scratch it. Just occasionally when someone told me what they would do if they could travel through time, I would take that TTA card out of my purse and hold it between my fingers and wonder. Was I the only one who felt like they were completely on their own? My Mam told me years before that that was what everyone thought. Perhaps though for a time traveller, it was more than just teenage angst. If I could meet other people who felt like me, then maybe I would feel less adrift from everything in my life.

For no reason other than an amusing diversion, I started to study early twentieth century German behind my mentor's back. I told myself that everyone needed a hobby and that it interested me. It was nothing to do with time travel. I had given that up for now.

Then I took a trip to early 1930s Germany.

*　*　*　*　*

I decided to learn from my trip to Aberdare in 1885 and give myself a chance by posing as a Welsh journalist working for the *Tarian y Gweithiwr* newspaper researching stories on the worker's lot in Germany for my editor in Aberdare. I would be an outsider but that would help excuse any mistakes in my German. During the 1930s, the Nazis tried to 'purify' the language of any American phrases and I was worried that I could have asked to use '*das telephone*' and immediately stood out compared to someone who used '*das fernsprecher*'. My purpose there was to find the TTA meeting.

When I arrived in Berlin, my wardrobe courtesy of the props department at my other job of course, I felt completely out of sorts again. I had left summer in Cardiff and yet arrived in winter in Berlin. It is hard to explain but if you are used to eating an evening meal while it is light, then to suddenly need to eat an evening meal while it is dark will completely mess with your digestive system and your sense of time. Druids may be right, we have more of a connection to nature than we realise.

My schoolgirl German got me a room in a small hotel, though visitors were rare of course. Again, that is another huge change. Most people do not realise that when Neville Chamberlain went to meet Hitler and sign the Munich Agreement in 1938, that was his first flight abroad. We take for granted now that we can fly around the world, but it was once the preserve of the rich only.

Frau Krause started out as the best host a time traveller could have. She wanted to know all about life in Britain and listened with interest to my tales of the coal mines of south Wales and the history of industrial unrest that had won the rights of the miners.

I made the silly mistake of talking about how my Dad had never forgiven Winston Churchill for his role in breaking up the miners' strike in Tonypandy. Frau Krause was confused as to why my Dad thought Churchill significant. I had to remind myself that in the early 1930s Winston Churchill was an MP with a sideline in lecture tours and writing, but not yet the war leader admired across some parts of the world, though not some households in south Wales.

Still, this proved to be to my benefit as Frau Krause took my interest in literature to be important to me and, to my delight, put in a word with a friend at the Ullstein publishing firm about whether they might want to talk to Fraulein Bowie and maybe publish some of her reflections on life in Germany.

I met Hermann Ullstein a few days later, he was lovely and yes, of course I told him. He was sitting in his office talking about the proud publishing history of his family firm and their respect for Britain, especially that we had once elected a Jewish Prime Minister. He talked about how Benjamin Disraeli had given hope to Jews around the world and noted that Mrs Disraeli had been Welsh. I pretended to know this, even though it was another detail left out of the history that we had been taught school. Then, having told myself that I would intervene as little as possible, I had to say something.

I explained to Herr Ullstein about the worsening economic situation in Germany and he nodded sadly at that. I talked about how the Nazis would take over everything and he gave an exasperated shrug. Then I said that they would attack the Jewish population in Germany and in every territory they conquered. Ullstein looked at me in what I thought was shock, a little confusion and then disbelief.

He could accept the Nazi desire for power, he could accept his own publishing company being taken over, but he could not accept the indiscriminate slaughter of millions. He argued that it made no sense. The Nazis would need a slave labour force in this expansive war that I was describing, they would not be able to afford to simply kill millions. I am not sure if his exasperation was because he disbelieved me or because he did not want to believe me.

Years later he did escape to the US, where he wrote a memoir about the 1930s in Germany. It is well worth reading, though he does not mention me or indeed, the Holocaust. I should not put them in that order! That is what happens to you as a time traveller, you become too convinced of your own power and significance. I left the Ullstein company and did not go back.

However, it was in Berlin that I met Oliver Wilkinson. I knew that his name was Oliver Wilkinson because it was written on his hand. I had to get the tram from Potsdamer Platz one Saturday and he was sitting opposite me. It was odd that he had an English name written on his hand and I wondered if it was the name of someone who he was meeting or whether it was his own name. Something told me that it was his own name and I could just see him, kind of owl-like, purchasing on the edge of a tram seat, sitting on a commuter train somewhere in the south-East of England with a lanyard around his neck saying that he worked in IT.

"*Sind Sie Engländer?*" I tried in my modest German.

"*Ja. Sie?*"

"*Eine Waliserin,*" I tried.

"Oh, whereabouts in Wales?" he asked, switching to English for the comfort of us both.

"Aberdare," I replied with home pride, "lots of green hills."

"Really? I thought that it was all industrial in those valleys. Don't get me wrong, I have great respect for the working class and the role they play in the war effort but ..."

Now we were at an impasse and I smiled. He knew that I was talking about a different Aberdare to the one that existed now

46

and I knew that he had just referenced a war that had not taken place yet. A look of panic spread over his cute face.

"I mean ... the first world war ... no, Great War. Dammit. Sorry, I'm just a bit confused," he stammered.

"First few days here, still got the time lag?" I asked, thinking that I sounded like a professional time traveller.

I could tell that he wanted to sigh and say 'yes' but he was on his guard.

"I'm Oliver Wilkinson," he said and I looked down at his hand, making him laugh.

"Written with a biro, a pen not widely available yet. Laszlo Biro's British patent is a few years away," I said with the confident smugness of a geek who had once had a bit part in a BBC Wales production.

"Patent was actually John Loud, I think - he invented the ball that gives the pen its name. Pretty standard pub quiz question, that one. I'm a geek too."

I smiled and extended my hand over to shake his, "Demerara Lee Bowie, what's with the naming your hand thing?"

Oliver looked surprised, "Question is more why you haven't done that. If you're one of us, I mean. It helps with the time lag ..."

He had paused to watch the reaction on my face. My heart took a few extra beats and I tried not to look as though I was swallowing hard. My silence and lack of surprise would tacitly confirm that I was 'one of us'. He looked nervous too though and I realised for the first time the danger of standing out as different, not just here but anywhere.

He continued, still watching my reaction carefully, "You need something that doesn't change or a phrase. I often write the date and cross off every 24 hours. It helps to adjust when you ... first arrive somewhere."

I had simply not thought of this! Of course, everything changed but why not write something that would ground you, a connection to your OTL? I smiled at him and he smiled at me, an unspoken agreement that we knew each other's secret. I blushed and looked away as if I was in a bad historical drama. Remember that I had been in quite a few by this point, both made for television and real ones.

"Are you here to stop me?" he asked and then, when I looked confused he added, "Clearly not – there are those out there who are dedicated to preserving the OTL - you know that's the original time line, right - and they will simply go around stopping people doing anything. So long as you're not one of those nuts on a 'let's kill Hitler' vibe then, that's fine."

Nervously, I fumbled in my purse and gave him a brief glimpse of the Time Travellers Anonymous card.

"Someone slipped it into my handbag in 1885," I whispered.

"I've heard of them, they always have their meetings here," he whispered back.

"Why?"

"Guess it's a convenient place for everyone to get to. Honestly, this city is crawling with people trying to ... well, you know ..."

Suddenly the lonely teenager who had become a lonely young adult had someone who was also from her species. If we ended up in bed together, it would not be because he thought that I was trying some 'I come from another time' chat-up line. I felt thrilled by the connection. My mind had to send out an immediate order for the rest of me to stay calm. That was an order that was not common in my life.

Oh I know, this is supposed to be all about scientific exploration but how often in life do you find yourself in 1930s Berlin with a stranger who turns out to be a time traveller like you? I am guessing that I am one of few people who can answer anything other than 'never' to that question.

48

He suggested we took the tram to a café he knew close to the park. He was clearly much more knowledgeable about Berlin than me so I tagged along and just nodded when he said things like, "The *Siegessäule* won't be quite where you are expecting it to be - it's smaller now too."

I warmed to his story as we walked to the café, He was from Trinity College, Dublin, though his accent betrayed him as English in origin. I was conscious that people might hear us and think that we stood out, so I kept quiet until we were in the café with coffee in front of us.

"In TCD," he explained, stirring his coffee idly and keeping his voice lowered, "the physics department has linked up with the history department and our mission is to gather accounts of Irish history from throughout time. We can't go back that far as we stand out too much, as I guess you did in 1885."

"I suppose I did. I thought that I was being careful," I replied, drinking my own coffee and feeling a little judged.

"An attractive young woman will always be noticed, it probably doesn't help."

I smiled at him and inwardly felt a little warmth at being called attractive. I did not acknowledge the compliment though, just swirled the coffee around a little faster with my spoon and avoided eye contact with him.

"Of course," he continued, "it's not for everyone. People become selfish when they have that kind of power. If you've been on a timeline where Tam O'Shanters are all the rage then that was the University of St Andrews boys messing with history. Then the Durham Uni guys tried to stop the Americans celebrating St Patrick's Day ... people end up doing silly things."

Like trying to stop their best friend emigrating, I thought. I was too embarrassed to admit that, so I teased him with, "You sound like a conspiracy theorist!"

"Not a theorist, but a conspiracy practitioner!" he announced proudly and too loudly as everyone else in the café stared at us, "Now come on, I've opened up to you here, what about the mysterious Demi Moore?"

"You're from a year when she's famous, then?" I asked with a laugh, "Wrong famous reference, but I'll take it that you are saying that I have movie star looks. Not much to tell - it's very different in Cardiff. We are part of the Physics Department and it is seen as a science project, I suppose. My supervisor warned me about trying to change history and ... I believe him. I am honestly a bit staggered that there are so many more of ... us."

I saw Oliver smile when I used the word 'us'. I could see that he was a lonely soul too and we were bonding over a sense of relief at being able to talk about these things.

"It sounds so lax though. What if someone tried to travel without paperwork? What if they tried to use time travel for their own selfish ends?"

Obviously I dodged that question, saying instead, "Tell me why you condemned people who want to kill ..."

I paused as I realised that discussing the murder of a leading politician in his own country was not going to count as blending in, so muttered "you know who."

Oliver looked around and I wondered who in that café might be watching us. I started to realise what it must be like to live in a society where you live in fear of being watched. I made a mental note never to complain about growing up in Aberdare again.

"Shall we go for a walk in the park?" he asked.

"I'd like that," I replied.

I would love to tell you about the trees or the bushes or the people who we passed on that afternoon, but I was more interested in questioning Oliver about his views on history.

Once we were out of earshot of anyone else walking in the park, he said calmly, "It seems crazy to have to say this but no-one seems to ask that question about killing ... you know who ... while pondering if taking another human life is justified."

Oliver removed his glasses and rubbed them on the inside of his jumper, as if this would make me see his point more clearly.

"It's not ... him, you see. He is our convenient excuse so that we don't have to think about the circumstances that produced him. We assume that he is evil through and through and that there was no possibility that he might have turned out differently in a different society.

Someone did kill him in a different timeline. Admiral Doenitz took over and the war was just as bloody. The Holocaust was signed off by a whole group of people, take away one of them and it still happened. It's the whole society that needs to change."

We paused under a tree that I did not recognise, but I felt that Oliver probably did. He reached up to a branch and gently folded a leaf in half, before letting go and watching the branch swing up again.

"I have found that people tend to assume that if you have the power to change something then you should do," I replied, "I suppose they see things in black and white. No-one wants the answer to a moral question to be 'it's not that simple'."

Oliver nodded, "How far do you want to go? Do you want to kill everyone around him? Take out the whole party? Do you want to go back and stop the first attempt to seize power? What about the economy – do you want to fix the economy in the hope that it will stop people being attracted to him? Do you want to change the end of the first war ... hell, do you want to get him into art school?"

We walked on in silence, the two of us thinking over what each other had said. As the path narrowed and we had to pass another couple walking the other way, I let my hand brush against his gently. I hoped that he might take it in his, but he just let a couple of fingers entwine with mine. It still felt exciting.

He did not look at me as we walked, but we kept this little connection down by our side. Eventually, I spoke, "Here's a mad thing that I have never told anyone before. When I was at school, I started this rumour that I had an oddly-shaped head. I thought that it would make me interesting."

Oliver stopped and turned to face me. Gently he raised his non-entwined hand up to my head and smoothed his fingers through my hair as if making the lightest check for any abnormal waves caused by bumps beneath. Normally I might have panicked over a man messing up my hair in this way, but I felt calm underneath this odd intimacy.

"Seems normal to me," he said, dropping his hand back down.

I wondered if people would be staring at us for such a display of intimacy in a public park. I had no idea. I had done no research on that. I could tell you that the English Garden in Munich is bigger than the *Tiergarten* in Berlin, but I have no idea if a man was allowed to stroke a woman's head in public.

"That's all I want," I said wearily, "I want to seem normal."

"You are interesting though, you're a time traveller."

"Which no-one will believe."

"Your name's Bowie."

"Which no-one believes either."

He hugged me and I pulled myself close into the hug as if hanging on to a buoy out in the ocean in the middle of a storm. We stood like that for a few moments until we both seemed to realise that the warmth might have looked out of place.

"It's odd though," said Oliver, breaking the hug and walking on, "look down that road there. You and I know that a wall will stand there and divide this city. We know that the dome on the Reichstag will fall and then rise again. We have mentioned that the *Siegessäule* is going to move and change size. We see the world differently to everyone else here."

I liked his use of the word 'we', I felt that we were two people who could share so much.

"I read - my mentor made me read - 'The Time Machine'," I said as we walked on towards an area where one day people would be shot for trying to move around their own city.

"That's nonsense though - it's about travelling forwards," replied Oliver, looking straight ahead.

"That's what I thought, but then I read it to the end. I mean, I read it again," I said, "what struck me is how nothing lasts forever. You're talking about the wall and the column and the dome and all that. It's not just them though, everything will go. All this travel, it makes me realise that everything is temporary. The traveller in that book, he notes that the stars have died."

Now Oliver reached over and held my hand as we walked. I held on to it and we continued in silence, not knowing enough about each other to know what the other was thinking but perhaps both considering how time travel gave us this insight into human impermanence.

He stopped, turned and looked at me, "Demi, I'm not sure how to say this but ..."

I took my other hand and put it to his lips. "Let's go to my hotel and discuss it there," I said in a voice that I hoped was more flirtatious than weary.

*   *   *   *   *

There is a reason that I am telling you all this. Other than Gary Sparrow in "Goodnight Sweetheart", I cannot think of any other time traveller who has been honest about their sex life. You probably would not ask most men about it, a girl in every century and all that. However, this was to prove my biggest mistake.

Not that there was anything wrong with Oliver. He was a sweet man, although I was rather hurt to wake up the next morning to find him clearing up his things to leave. I knew that he had history to observe and I had to find my TTA meeting. I had felt normal around him and thought that we would meet again, but I only realised that it was a mistake when Frau Krause knocked on my door a little while after Oliver had left.

I probably did not help matters by answering the door wrapped in a dressing gown and I could see Frau Krause take a slight step backwards when I did.

Frau Krause apologised profusely, barely looking me in the eyes as she did so. The trouble was that she had noticed that I had had a late night caller, a gentleman caller and when she had asked him if he was my husband, he had said no. Fiancé she might have accepted if the wedding day was soon, but an overnight caller with no connection, well that was a different matter.

I could have interrupted and tried to defend myself, even with my standard of German, but Frau Krause was in full flow. It was not about her, she re-assured me. Although she was not one of those who approved of such things, she did know that we had been living through liberal times and sometimes a young woman could be prey to temptations. No, she did not blame me but she had a reputation to keep. When people started to say that Frau Krause's was the place to go to meet a certain kind of young woman, then everything would be lost. Did I understand that it was not personal?

My translation was only filling in parts of this, but luckily she repeated herself often and spoke slowly in parts either because she knew that I might struggle to understand or because she was unsure of the right words through politeness rather than linguistic shortfall. She paused after the question about whether I had considered what would happen if I was pregnant?

I assured her that there was no chance of pregnancy. Frau Krause's face filled with concern and she told me that that was what a young man always said '*das erste Mal*' ... the first time.

I decided to accept the implied suggestion that I was naïve rather than immoral and simply nodded as if I was being taught a great lesson. This was not enough to save my place though and I was asked to gather up my things and leave by nightfall.

Nightfall. When I could see stars that would one day die too. I nodded and said, "Not even the stars survive."

Frau Krause stared at me and so I started to ask, "*Haben Sie 'The Time Machine' ge ...*" but stopped.

*　*　*　*　*

"And that is why no-one has ever killed Hitler," concluded Demi, signalling to the conference organiser at the back of the room that she needed another glass of water, "because they are too busy seducing other time travellers."

She waited to see how many of them were still awake and there was a polite ripple of laughter in reaction to her self-depreciation. She could see a junior member of conference staff appear at the back of the room with a jug of water. At least some things were working.

"No, the message is that it is morally questionable and also that you soon learn to appreciate that history is complex."

The assistant brought the jug of water to the podium and Demi refilled her glass. A hand went up in the front row.

"What happened to Oliver?" asked a man who looked as though he had only been sent to this conference because no-one else in his department wanted to go.

"Oh, he was the man who shot Hitler."

Part 5

Demi pressed another button on the pad in front of her and now the picture behind her was of a group of people dancing in a field. The title was 'Travelling for Pleasure'.

"I have just one more story to tell you, I promise," she said, "I really want to emphasise to you how un-glamorous time travel is and how over time the danger and the inconvenience and the mental confusion reach a point where you want to stop. There are very few old time travellers, with good reason."

There was a sound from the room outside the main conference hall. That would be lunch being delivered and the audience would know it. From now on, most of them would be focussed on their technique for getting to the table before the cheese ran out. You could invite people to the most in-depth and high-powered conferences but, when asked if the conference was any good, they would tell you about the lack of coleslaw. She was now in a race against time, a thought that amused her. No, she decided, she would reframe it as being in a race against coleslaw. That made more sense.

Demi looked down at her hand. Written on it was 'Demi Bowie' and 'Where are we now?'

*   *   *   *   *

Of course I passed my Masters. My Dad had told me frankly that by now he had given up on me getting a proper job but Mam had put another photo of me in a graduation gown on the mantelpiece. I secured a grant that would pay for me to enrol for a PhD and asked Professor Leeds to be my PhD supervisor. Officially I was looking at an obscure area of physics that only he and I understood but unofficially we were studying time lag and how the body can be better conditioned to survive travelling through time.

In the rest of my time, I taught the undergraduates and I was an extra in historical dramas at the weekend. I even had enough money to rent a small flat in the Cardiff suburb of Roath and let Mam and Dad wave me tearful and stoic goodbyes respectively every time I ended a visit to them.

I will admit that nights out and even seeing my friends and family became rarer the longer I studied. My time away from Aberdare – both in the present in Cardiff and also further afield in places like Berlin – meant that I no longer sounded quite like my school friends and my career meant that we had less in common. I was also developing a distrust of the present.

I had no more grand ideas of changing my life or changing the world, I just enjoyed being somewhen else for a change. When you live around time travel, you become used to it as being as mundane as someone hopping off to Athens for the weekend for some winter sun. It is just that with me it was Athens in 1974. It is the only way to guarantee good holiday weather.

I had learned that when I arrived somewhere new, I had to know two things. Who I was – hence my name on my hand – and also where I was. You might think that *when* I was would be more important, but you will notice that my excess of memories means that I am vague about dates. It is hard to say 'this happened two years after I was twenty-one years old' if I have four years of memories between twenty-one and twenty-three years old. The one constant was the storeroom. If I could remind myself that I was in a store room in the university building on Newport Road, Cardiff then I would be fine. That is why I always wrote, 'Where are we now?' on my hand.

Leeds was having health issues and was in and out of university, so I was left to my studies for the most part. With no-one but the accountant monitoring the university's electricity bills likely to find out, travel became a way of hiding. Others in the department did travel too, but they were under strict conditions and for academic purposes only. Time travel was generally regarded by those who knew about it as about as dangerous as the early days of flight. We were the trick acrobats of the physics world!

I did keep the TTA card but I did not go back to Berlin. It seemed to prove to me that travelling to anywhere that you were not familiar with was going to be a problem.

Perhaps I was using time travel as a way of hiding from the present, you would have to ask a psychologist to explain that rather than me, but as my PhD went on, so my travelling increased again. I was not addicted I told myself, I was just doing it a lot.

As for Oliver? Okay, I was joking about him shooting Hitler. Sometimes time travellers just like to mess with your sense of reality too. Did I try to contact him back in the present? Yes, I did.

How can I explain it? After weeks of putting it off, I finally plucked up the courage to call TCD and ask to speak to Oliver Wilkinson in the history department. They told me that there was no such person working there. Perhaps they were nervous about giving out personal details, I thought. I know what you are thinking and no, it never occurred to me that he might have been lying about his name - it had been written on his hand, after all!

I searched online and found no references to him at TCD. His name was common enough that he could have been one of a hundred online references and not even me with my low level work rate could justify time researching each one.

Then the shock came. I had left my name and number with TCD's history department and to my huge surprise, one rainy Monday when I was staring out of the Physics Department window at a brick wall, they phoned.

Nuala Fahey wanted to know if I was the person who could speak to them about Oliver Wilkinson. I said that I had wanted to talk to him and we both seemed confused. There was a little back and forth and then she asked if I was the person who was supplying his reference.

It all became clear and when I say clear, I mean that it became excessively complicated. I took out a piece of paper from the departmental printer and wrote a fact at the top - Oliver had only just applied for his postdoctoral study at TCD. Did that mean that he had been from further forwards in the future than me? I thought that the physics were pretty squarely on the side of you only being able to travel from this day backwards. However, if this day had already happened for him and he was then a couple of years ahead ...

I scratched my head, I rubbed my nose, I tore up the piece of paper and tried again. If I went back from 2019 to 1932 and met someone who had come back from - say 2010 - would they not have seen me as someone from the future? If I told them about the London Olympics of 2012, would I be revealing a future that they could then change?

I ripped up the next piece of paper ... and the next one. The one after that was soon in a ball next to the departmental recycling bin too. I sat back and swore under my breath softly. There had to be a logical explanation as to why Oliver had not contacted me!

Addicot walked past and gave me a cheery wave and a slight smile of recognition at my dramatic frustration.

"Difficult theory you are working on there, Demerara?" he called over.

"Just ... it does not make sense," I said, quickly scrunching up the next piece of paper as I realised that I was halfway to drawing two hills on the top of the 'v' of 'Oliver'.

"There is always a rational answer, you know that. Are you coming to the canteen? Leeds is back in today and he is holding forth about his glory days in the swinging sixties and I want to distract him by throwing peanuts at him!"

I shook my head wearily. There was no point telling Leeds about my dilemma with Oliver. He would probably say something stupid like that Oliver had lied to me in Berlin and that he did not want to see me again. I could find no rational explanation but I also knew that my best form of escape from a lack of rational explanations lay in the store room. I fancied another idyllic sunny day in the never ending summer of 1976.

*   *   *   *   *

It was a couple of years into my PhD that Professor Leeds announced that he was retiring due to his ill-health. I was sad, of course, but who could blame him for wanting to retire and forget that he had ever sat in front of students who had not even opened the course textbook but still expected to pass the exam? I had to admit that I had become fond of his guidance, much as I liked to still think that I rebelled against it.

In those couple of years of my PhD Leeds had developed that reputation as being an entertaining speaker in the canteen with Addicott as his constant good-hearted source of heckling.

Most of the men in the department were on Addicott's side. Leeds's colleagues simply could not believe that a man who looked like a somnambulant heron could have had the wild side described in his stories. With the announcement of his retirement, Addicott finally challenged Leeds to prove it and in any normal place of work there would have been a hunt for photographs, old girlfriends or witness statements. This was not a normal place of work.

When it came to settling a bet, both thought it ideal to turn to time travel. It was Addicott, who said that I, as the only woman in the department, should be the one to judge, given that I knew about 'what made men attractive'. I had no idea where that comment came from but I watched with surprise as Leeds agreed and proposed that I travelled to the mid-60s to find him at a university party that he attended in London and to bring back my own conclusions. A small sum of money was wagered, but academic pride seemed more important.

"Where am I going, Professor?" I asked as I stood in his office for what I realised would probably be one of the last times.

"Please, call me Gareth, we've reached that point after all these years, I think," he replied and he pointed to the picture of the house and the framed bus ticket on his desk. These would be my directions.

If I was going to fit into Swinging London then I was going to need to know what kind of music people listened to, what kind of language they used and all those other little details that would help. Leeds had studied at King's College and I pored over all sources of its buildings, its students and the history of the period. A month later and with all my research done, I was feeling groovy - and not in a 21st century ironic way.

I set my date to travel to – 21st July 1965. I would arrive in the storeroom in Cardiff and then take a train over to London and try to find the party that Leeds had been so specific about.

"Stones or Beatles?" asked Addicott to test me.

"Kinks," I replied.

"You're okay for tomorrow?" asked Leeds.

"Sure, I've done this before," I said with a smile that hid that I was touched by his concern.

"I've packaged up a few things for you," he said, his voice even more insistent and serious than normal and not fitting with a frivolous academic bet, "I have placed it in the ... you know, I have never embraced calling it a 'time machine'. Anyway, you must keep it in there, it's things I need to know, even if the timeline changes."

"Okay," I replied, "And I have the bag here with the location of the party, the bus ticket and a couple of other things."

We looked at each other for a few moments and I had a feeling that he wanted to say more, but did not know how to say it.

"This is about more than settling things with Addicott, isn't it?" I asked.

"Let's just say, this trip has been set up for a while. Now go and get a good night's sleep, that time lag will only get worse as you get older."

"Yes, Sir!" I said with a mock salute and left him in his office. I paused at the door, feeling as though there was something more that I should say as well, but could not find the words either.

I was, as ever, bending the truth for my mentor when I agreed to go straight home because my first port of call was the pub across the road, The Fellow Traveller. It was one of those modern pubs that tries too hard to be historic. I have always loved those, they show people in the present are desperate to be in the past. I can tell you from experience that the past is not as good as you think it was.

I sipped slowly on a cool pint. Leeds's retirement and his extra seriousness made it feel as though something final was happening. I had the details of the party and how to get there in my coat pocket, I would pick up some extra clothes and some money tomorrow.

It was then that my phone rang and I perked up when I saw that it was Georgie phoning. I had not seen much of her over the previous few months and as she said that she and Sarah were in the city and wanted to talk to me, I ordered another pint and waited for their arrival.

Thinking about it, I knew very little about Sarah. Beyond that her job was something in Ebbw Vale and that her middle name was Alvara - and I only found that out at the wedding - I knew very little. I should have used my time travel to do some due diligence. Imagine that, I could go to when they first met and work out if she was genuinely falling in love or just eyeing up a new chance. I could check that Georgie was not pushed into marriage, I could ... I could be the over-protective friend. If my Georgie non-time in Australia had taught me anything, it should have been that I had to let other people make decisions for themselves.

Mrs and Mrs Evans arrived a little while after and Georgie went to the bar to buy a new pint for me, a double vodka for Sarah and a lemonade for herself. She must have driven down, I thought. You learn to make these quick deductions as a time traveller. It also struck me that Georgie had put on weight since we last met, which must have been that 'happiness spread' that they talk about when people are in a happy relationship and not watching what they eat.

Sarah looked a lot like I remembered her. Her dark blonde hair had grown longer, her clothes were still all colours of purple and pink and she looked like she was embracing what I noticed magazines had called the 'hippy revival'. I smiled because I was trying to remember whether tomorrow's trip would enable me to meet any actual hippies to find out if these endless revivals were at all genuine.

"Not wearing a Tam O'Shanter?" I quipped.

"What's a Tam O'Shanter?" replied Sarah, flipping a beer mat between her fingers.

"You used to ... oh maybe you didn't anymore, I get confused."

"How many of those have you had?" she replied with a laugh.

Georgie returned from the bar and there was a strange silence and a look that passed between the two wives.

"What?" I asked.

"I have to tell you," said Georgie, with a gasp of air that showed her excitement, "I'm pregnant."

Sarah leaned over and took Georgie's hand in hers, "We're expecting a baby."

"Oh Georgie! That's fantastic! Oh, come over here and give me a hug!" was my response and to thank goodness that I lived in an age where not only could two women get married but they could bring up a child too.

"I know we haven't been around much but ... err ... I'm three months gone now, so it's time to tell people," my friend confirmed.

"I've started painting the nursery," added Sarah proudly.

"I've so wanted to tell you, Demi-L ..."

"Three months? Oh, you should have told me!" I said, a raised eyebrow having stopped Georgie hyphenating my name.

She should have told me. Once upon a time this kind of momentous news, let alone that they were going into the process to have a child, would have been something that we would have discussed. I felt rather sad about this. I know that it is natural, but my friend being that bit further away from me felt a little like I had felt as a child when she was going to be ten thousand miles away from me.

"Well, it's been a bit of a process, so we were waiting until we were three months gone," said Sarah, giving Georgie's hand a squeeze.

"Well, *llongyfarchiadau* as we say in Welsh," I said, raising my glass and taking a long drink of beer.

"We'd like you to be the child's godmother," said Georgie once my pint glass had returned to the table.

"Oh wow," I replied, suddenly imagining a future as the crazy aunt who takes the child on inappropriate adventures that somehow end up being educational, "I would be honoured. Honestly, honoured."

"You could be the brainy aunt who teaches our child all about science and stuff," said Georgie, not quite seeing how I saw my role in her child's life.

At this point, the excited conversation became background noise for a moment while I realised something truly life-changing. I had something to live for in the future. My life until this point had been all about the past, but this child was something for the future. Tomorrow's trip might have to be my last.

"Don't worry," said Sarah, reaching over and placing her other hand on mine so that all three of us were momentarily linked, "there's someone out there for you, I'm sure, you just haven't met him yet."

The conversation through the next pint was all about babies. It was hardly a surprise that Georgie's mind was taken up with this now and that Sarah was making plans for how they would support the child.

"We haven't told her parents yet," cautioned Sarah, making me feel a bit more special, "we don't know how they might be."

I nodded my agreement and thought how sad that was for Georgie.

"Oh you will forgive us if we don't call her Demi-Lee or Demerara, won't you?" asked Georgie and I almost snorted beer out of my nose laughing at that suggestion!

"Seriously, it's going to be such a big thing for us," she added, "but I am reading all the magazines. You think that I am a bit ridiculous sometimes, but I can be serious and this lovely woman here can be a bit ditzy too."

"Really?" I said, giving Sarah a look to say that I had never realised that she had such hidden shallows.

"Yes, just the other day I found that she had written her own name on her hand! How silly is that! And worse, I think that I had spotted that before! How can you forget your own name?"

I felt the colour drain from my face and I saw Sarah see my reaction. I also saw that it was not a surprise to her. There is only one reason why someone habitually writes their own name on their hand and it is not ditziness.

"Ooo, you'll have to excuse me, I need the toilet again," said Georgie, rising carefully as if she had an eight month bump to protect, "I'm practising for incontinence after childbirth, clearly."

Georgie reached down and planted a kiss on Sarah's cheek and then walked to the toilet. Sarah and I were both clearly calculating how long we needed before Georgie was out of ear shot. I started.

"Your name written on your hand, eh? Now why would that be?" I asked .

"Don't know what you mean," she said, draining the last drop of vodka from her glass.

"You know what I mean. Are you messing with her timeline, that's all I want to know."

"Like you stopped her moving to Australia?"

There was a pause full of anger and both of us tried to give each other mean looks and probably failed, given the amount of alcohol that we had drunk.

"Who are you?" I demanded.

"I am the world's first female time traveller!" Sarah declared proudly.

"No, you're the second. I'm the first."

"I don't think so," she said and her smugness annoyed me even more.

"Besides, there was a book about one in the 1960s, a wrinkled person who went in time and then a woman who had a dog more recently. You can't be more than the third or fourth and behind me at any rate."

Youthful bluff is a strange thing. When Professor Leeds told me that I was not the first female time traveller, I bent the facts so that I could deny them. However, now that the facts supported me, I suddenly believed them wholeheartedly, even if I could not remember them completely.

Sarah leaned forwards as if she was letting me in on something that might surprise me, "I work for an outsourcing company in Ebbw Vale that specialises in ... private contract work. It's not just universities involved in this. Georgie doesn't need to know," she replied calmly.

"It's immoral. You shouldn't mess with a 'stationary'."

"And so you academics can sit in judgement on the rest of the world? It is immoral but that is why we are members of a partnership known as The New Luddites. We aim to destroy all the world's time travel machinery. We'll find yours and get it too, one day."

It was going to take a little while for me to take this in. How long had she known? Had she messed with my timeline? Was she only exploiting Georgie? I became drunkenly fiercely protective of my best friend once again.

"Did you see her in Australia? Do you think that she was happier growing up there?"

"That's why we have to stop this technology. Though I might have changed a few things here or there. Just to stop her suffering."

"That's abuse. You have to let people make their own decisions."

"Do you know how hard it has been for your friend to get pregnant? Do you know the disappointments we would have had? You want her to suffer?"

This was the same argument that I had wrestled with all those years ago or a few years ago if you had not travelled in time. I was fed up with having it.

"I'll tell her," I threatened.

"You wouldn't. Besides, I'd just go back in time to make sure the two of you never met."

"Then I would go back in time further to make sure that you two never met."

This is the kind of argument that time travellers have. I am sorry to say that it lacks any intellectual sophistication. Luckily, we soon fell back on a more traditional way of solving our dispute when I stood up and shouted, "You are going to stop or I will make you so sorry that you got messed up in this!"

Sarah stood up and yelled, "You try to make me!"

She then took a drunken swing at me with her fist. I do not think that either of us had any experience of fighting and it really showed. Her fist swung a foot away from my face and she fell to one side. However, I leant back to avoid it and lost my balance. As she fell to one side and I fell to the other, I reached over and grabbed on to her hair for balance. It pulled her the wrong way and she shrieked. Trying to steady herself, she grabbed at me, caught the shoulder of my dress and ripped it across one side.

"This is one of my favourite dresses!" I lied.

"Doesn't surprise me," she said with a shrug of contempt.

Having fought ineffectively, we were both suddenly aware of Georgie coming out of the toilets. As if she was the glowing beacon of sanity in both our lives, we quickly sat down again and pretended to be finishing our drinks.

"And that's why Doctor Who is fundamentally flawed as a concept," said Sarah, as if she had been caught mid-sentence by Georgie's return.

"You and I know that time travel is impossible," I replied.

"Oh God, sci-fi chat! I forgot that you two had that in common. I'll go and get another round," said Georgie.

"No Georgie, I'm sorry, I have to go," I said, standing up and grabbing my coat from the back of the chair.

"Ooo why, we wanted to have a catch up, didn't we Sarah?"

"I think that perhaps the two of us have drunk enough, darling. Let's all call it a night."

With that we hugged and somehow Georgie managed not to notice my torn dress or the clump of her girlfriend's hair that was missing.

Part 6

I walked straight to the university building and let myself in with a swipe of my ID card. I was not thinking straight, I was full of a kind of anger and annoyance that even gaining the powers of a godmother could not assuage. I just did not want to be in the present anymore and I knew how to deal with that. This one could even be on work time!

I walked straight into the storeroom and into the time travel machine and set it working. Before long I was in a storeroom over forty years in the past. Okay, it sounds a lot less dramatic than I had hoped, not least because the storeroom door was locked from the outside. It took what felt like an hour of shouting and banging on that door before a security guard let me out. He made no comment. He was used to strange people coming out of that room - a red-faced woman wearing a torn dress and smelling of beer was one of the saner things he had seen.

In my anger, I had forgotten my planning and I had no money. Somehow I needed to replace my torn dress and get to a party in east London by the weekend. I had the directions and the bus number and I was too stubborn to admit that I needed to go back for anything. Time travel had already made me resourceful, now it had to make me a criminal.

Looking out of the front door of the department building, I could see that there were fewer cars outside than in my present and the air tasted strangely different. The real change though was how many buildings were unfamiliar. The hotel was gone and the student flats and the car park ... this was clearly the same road that the university building stood on, but it was one of the few buildings that I recognised.

Of course, in 1965 I could go and see the Victorian era Queen Street station before it was demolished. Then there would be the remains of Greyfriars friary which would also be knocked down to be replaced by a dull office block before the 1960s were over! For a minute the unfamiliarity seemed quite exhilarating, but only for a minute. It was dark, I was drunk and I had no money. I had to improve the odds.

I knew that I had to keep calm and remember what I was doing. I looked at my hand. I was Demi and 'where are we now' was in Cardiff. The prison would be in the same place. Bute Terrace would be in the same place. The Golden Cross pub and then the Customs House … if I could follow the old landmarks that I knew from the future then they would take me to the central station. Luckily Cardiff Central station … no, it would be called Cardiff General station in 1965 … had been in the same place ever since Brunel decided to move the river Taff to make room for it in the city centre.

If I could find the station, then that would be at the end of St Mary's Street. I was going to have to hope that the security systems of the past were not as good as the ones I knew and throw a brick through the window of Howells department store and steal a dress. I could then go back to the university building, wait for the next day and then after the sun had risen again, make my next move.

You can tell from this description that I was seriously time lagged. My mind and body felt out of place and I was, of course, still several pints along the way from somewhere in the future. I had forgotten that returning to the university building from my dress-stealing raid, I would find the door shut and my ID card a piece of technology that had not been invented yet. I think that I sat on the steps of the building for an hour, freezing and crying before a security guard appeared. Luckily it was the security guard who had seen me emerge from the storeroom earlier and he let me in. It was one of the saner requests etc.

Once inside, I took off a shoe and tried to prise open a desk drawer in reception with the heel – what can I say, I was not yet taking my own advice to wear comfortable shoes for time travel. The second locked drawer that I smashed open contained the cash box and that came open with a little more violence using a chair leg. I would have to remember to reimburse the university with a donation of a fee from a conference presentation or something in the future.

After some violence, a little theft and a few hours sleep, I was ready to head to London.

* * * * *

I might have been drunk, nauseous and a violent criminal, but I had a new dress and a party to find. Despite everything, I was still determined to fulfil my mission. I owed it to my PhD supervisor. Enough money came from the university petty cash box to get me on a train to London and I just had to feign being a foreign tourist to explain why all the money looked unfamiliar and why I did not understand words like 'shilling'.

It is also funny that unlike with Cardiff, I had no real desire to see how London had changed. Perhaps the rows of Victorian terraces around Paddington station would still look the same, minus the satellite dishes and recycling bins. I did laugh at the tube map without the Jubilee line on it, let alone the Docklands or Overground lines.

Suffice to say, I had enough money for the train ticket, a sandwich by the Thames and a tip for the kind man in the newsagents who told me how to get to the party address. Actually, I will be honest and tell you that I fell asleep on the Circle Line and it was only after being woken up and told to move on for the third time that I felt at least awake enough to head for the party.

My technique was going to be blagging through and through. As I say, time travel had made me resourceful. When I reached the house, I simply stood back from the door, tried to look disinterested and said, "Yeah, David said that this was where it was happening." The guy who had opened the door clearly did not care who I was, who I claimed to know or my explanation of anything and he let me in.

The noise coming from inside and the smell of drink and other substances on the wind told me that this was the place to find Professor Leeds – Gareth, as I remembered he would be now. There is a survival instinct that kicks in when you travel and I had it in spades. This mission should now be easy – find Professor Leeds, decide if he was cool or not and then head home and work out how to deal with Sarah.

The venue might have been the small, suburban house in the photograph but there were student-age partygoers packed in everywhere I could see. Everything was bright and loud and I started to wonder how I was going to find Leeds. A woman who had clearly been there far too long spotted me looking lost, grabbed my hand and took me over to a thin man in the corner with a faraway look.

"He's in the band!" she said excitedly.

"Are you in a band?" he asked me.

I offered my hand and he shook it awkwardly and then glimpsed the writing on it.

"Demerara Lee Bowie," I said, feeling the need to be formal.

"And why do you have 'where are we now' written on your hand, Bowie?" he asked.

"It's a travel thing. It kind of reminds you where you are … err … it's a Berlin thing. I started it there."

"Berlin?" he said, letting my hand go but looking interested in talking more.

"Yeah look, I am trying to find my friend – Gareth … Gary Leeds. Do you know him?"

73

"Gary? Yeah, he's in the back room over there, should have known."

I walked away with a forced smile but only made it a few feet before the woman who had grabbed my hand approached me.

"You know who that is, right?" she asked, "They were playing earlier – Davie Jones and the Lower Third. They've got a single out!"

"I prefer the Kinks," I said with a shrug.

Luckily, this set her off into a scream of 'you really got me' and I was able to move on. I know that you are probably looking for observations of the 1960s and music and fashion and so on, but to be honest I was just looking to settle a bet and go home. I was on a mission. I also realised that being on a mission had been the definition of my life too. This was who I was and, other than the man that I was about to meet, there had been no-one else who had understood that. Except Oliver and I did not want to dwell on that, I just wanted to complete my mission.

I stumbled into the back bedroom of the little house and there was the oddest sight you could imagine. It was the man who I knew as a sleepy Professor, but this version was looking remarkably fit, full of energy, dark-haired and so alive. Next to him on a row of beanbags and snuggled under his arms were two young women, looking like they were hanging on his every word. It was such a contrast to the man who I knew that I forgot all my research.

"Professor!" I shouted.

He started to reply with some kind of joke about them sending in too many girls for him, but then I saw his face change to one of both understanding and amazement.

"Professor? I make Professor! Wow! Hey sorry, I didn't expect they'd send a girl."

"Woman," I corrected him once more or for the first time, depending on how you viewed it.

"Oh right, whatever, I ... girls, can you go and play somewhere else for a moment?"

The two young women looked annoyed and shot me glances of annoyance as they pushed past me out of the room.

"Sorry," he said again, "it's probably a different era to yours. Is it? Where are you from? 1986? 1997? No, don't tell me!"

I was still staring at his black hair. He had a ridiculously colourful shirt too and there was dark hair sprouting over the top button. I think that he had won his future bet, but his greeting now intrigued me more. First things first, though.

"Don't worry, I've read Germaine Greer. She said that the 1960s gave a woman the right to say yes, but took away her right to say no."

"What?"

"You're fine, just don't blame me when hashtag MeToo comes along."

"Sit, sit!" he said, patting a beanbag, "But don't tell me too much, although perhaps how you smoke a 'hashtag'?"

I sat on the beanbag and did so with a fall that was heavier than I expected and I almost toppled over backwards. They were not a stable way of sitting and I realised why they had never truly gained mass appeal as a substitute for a chair.

"You were expecting me then?" I asked to clear up my next problem with the situation.

"Yes, here," he said, taking out a rolled cigarette and offering it to me.

"No."

"Mind if I do?"

"Indoors?"

"Where else?"

I pulled a face that showed how uncomfortable I was and he shook his head and put the cigarette in the top pocket of his shirt. I could tell that he wanted to ask me about this, but he was fighting a thought-out principle not to ask anyone from the future about the future. The fact that I was talking to someone who was okay with me being from another time was a little bit of a head spin and this was on top of the time lag and the unstable bean bag. It was a good head spin though.

"Okay then," he said, looking a little more earnest and a little bit more like the somnambulant heron of his future, "I have been working on time travel for a few years. It's actually pretty straightforward once you realise that you only travel in time and not space and ..."

"You have to take the equipment with you – yes, I know, I discovered it too, though I did read your research, of course."

"Yes, yes, of course, I'm ... sorry, you're the first person I have met who ... anyway. I built a prototype and tried it out earlier this week. Or was it last week?"

I laughed. Professor Leeds was sitting forwards on the beanbag with his hands clasped together, trying to understand a process that I had more experience of than he did. This would be like a lecture, I thought.

"Those are two of the side effects," I said with a confidence that I enjoyed, "you stop being able to remember anything as a linear progression of events and you feel kind of disconnected from your own experience for a few days like jet lag ... though ... err ... jet lag may not be an easy one to explain to a lot of people here yet."

At this point a man burst into the room, shouted something that we both found it hard to decipher, looked at us both, mumbled 'breadheads' and stumbled out, banging the door behind him loudly.

"So, why here, now, this party – what's the significance?" I asked.

"Earlier tonight I decided that if I published the research then I would leave it for ten years, maybe twenty years and then ask the best and brightest of the time travel brigade – we have a brigade, surely? – to come back and tell me how it worked out. The research is yet to be published. Should I do it? Do we use this technology to make the world a better place? Why have I still heard of Adolf Hitler?"

"Ah yes, the Hitler thing is a bit more complicated. Ask a historian, I haven't got time. I'll be honest with you Prof, I don't think much of it. It's not as dramatic or heroic as the books about it claim."

"Ha!" said Leeds, clapping his hands together, "You know what, I just bought a copy of last year's edition of 'The Time Machine' by H.G.Wells? Have you ...?"

He stopped speaking as he saw the weariness in my face. I sighed a deep sigh, raised my eyebrows and he knew that he had talked about it at length in the future.

"Ah, okay," he said, "it's just weird to meet someone who knows what I am talking about."

"There are others," I replied, "Others have copied it too."

Leeds jumped up and started to pace about the small room, which was hard when the floor was strewn with beanbags, but he stepped over them with big strides that made him look even more like a heron.

"There's the team in Ireland, I know about them. Another in Switzerland and St Andrews, their university has been after the same grants for years ... lots of places actually except the USA.

They're pouring all their money into trying to land on the moon. That's crazy, isn't it?"

I looked away from eye contact and hummed to myself. If he was fishing for information about the future now, I was not going to play his game.

"Yes," he continued, "but they are all going to take from my research, I am sure of it. If I destroy the research then they would never do it. Are there many people travelling?"

"Sit down, please," I said, "you're making me dizzy with your pacing. Yes, there are quite a few. I have even found that there are those dedicated to stopping it."

Professor Leeds sat down heavily on to a beanbag and almost toppled over backwards. Okay, so that was not a skill people in 1965 had either. He righted himself and then looked at me rather sadly.

"I have other things to study, I was just sure that this was the thing ... is it really never used for good?"

I realised that he was the only man who could hear my confession. Of all the trips and the travellers and the people around me, my academic mentor had been the one who I should have been honest with.

"When I first used it," I said, swallowing hard and looking straight ahead at some garish wallpaper, "I did it to stop my best friend emigrating."

"And did it ... did it work?" he asked excitedly.

I turned to face him and only some odd idea of professionalism stopped a tear growing any bigger in each eye.

"It's not about whether it works or not, it's about how it's used. My first thought was to be selfish. Then I tried to change things for other people and that was no more than trying to be the saviour of the world too. I met a man ..."

My voice trailed off and he put an arm on my shoulder. A man who had been so confident with young women earlier seemed awkward around one who was bearing her soul.

"No-one was going to believe me anyway," he sighed.

We sat there for a while, the sound of the music blaring outside and shouts and giggles forcing their way through the door at us. It was only in the silence that something struck me.

"Hold on," I said, "time travel has been my life. Without it ... I don't have anything. It's been my mission. If you destroy your research then I never read it, I never meet you, I never travel here and ... am I stuck here?"

"You would lead an alternative life. You could be a doctor or an architect or something."

"I want to be me. I don't want that to be changed by someone else's decision. That was what went wrong with that first trip. If there's not time travel, then I suppose that no-one would become a time traveller, but this has been all that there has been in my life since age ten."

What kind of a life would I go back to? Where would I be? What would I do? Would I still be about to become a godmother? Georgie would not be married to a time traveller at least, but what if they had never met? As for me, I would never have known that this life was possible. It was like a kind of death and I felt sick.

"You can't," I added in a whisper.

Professor Leeds was looking at me with some sympathy. He was mulling over dilemmas that I had spent years addressing. Luckily, he had an answer.

"I'll destroy all my research while you are here. The world will change, but you will still be here. Then you can take my prototype," he said, "take it back to your time and I will meet you there and destroy it with you. Will that work? You'll know two time lines ... or will everything revert to the new one?"

"No, from my experience, I'll still be me, but with another life of memories to cope with," I replied, "but I have to be able to make one other trip first. There is something I need to make sure happens."

"You need to make sure you meet your husband or something?"

I smiled for the first time and shook my head, "I think that I owe a favour to someone. What about you though? If you don't travel, then you'll never know what adventures you might have had. You never told me much about them."

"Hmm," he said, scratching where he would one day have no more than a white mop of hair, "Didn't I think of that? I could have given you something to bring back so that it ..."

Leeds stopped speaking because I was laughing. Of course, that was what he had put into the machine for me to travel back with. He guessed that I would advise against publishing the research, so he was sending himself the story of what happened in his other life.

With that, the man who I had known until this day as a reserved academic and a respected teacher, stood up, threw open the door to the main party room and yelled, "Hey girls! I'm a time traveller, who wants to know what life is like on Pluto?"

I was going to enjoy telling him off for this in the future.

* * * * *

And that is how I came to be stepping out of a time travel machine prototype in 2019 to find Leeds waiting for me. It was odd seeing him as an old man so soon after seeing him as a young man, but something of that young spark lay there behind the eyes. I wish that I had taken the trouble to see it before. He was leaning on an axe, though I imagined that he did not have the strength to wield it himself.

80

I took the axe from him and laid it down next to the machine. Then I stepped forward and hugged him.

"Woah! I'm the one who hasn't seen this version of you in years!" he said.

I let go of him and nodded, "We're the only two now, then?"

"We are. As far as I know, there are still time travel research projects, but they have none of them cracked it. Mind you, the Americans did make it to the moon."

"Though some people doubt that."

"Welcome to a world where everyone will doubt your achievements."

"I'm a woman in academia, that's my life already."

"You stopped off in the last decade to run that errand you said needed doing, then?" he asked, ignoring my sarcasm.

I could tell that he was digging for information, but I knew that I had done what I needed to do, so I just smiled and nodded.

He continued : "One other thing ... I don't know how to put this. One of the reasons I don't think that we - people - should travel in time is that you couldn't put me in my twenties next to me in my seventies, y'know, they're ... well, how can I say?"

"You were a dick when you were twenty. I saw that. You aren't now, it's okay."

Professor Leeds shuffled nervously on the spot, suddenly seeming to have the mannerisms of a younger man, "We didn't treat women ... well ... I have had a lot of time to regret some of the things I did back then."

I placed an arm on his arm to re-assure him and said, "Of course, you do realise that the irony was that all those women you tried to impress by saying that you were a time traveller, they would all have doubted you, at least a little. The only one who wouldn't have doubted you is the one who would never have been impressed."

Professor Leeds laughed and said, "I'm glad it was you. It has been a long wait, but I am glad that it was you."

"But it never happened ... well, not in this timeline, surely?"

Leeds nodded his head, "No, but I have had great times reading through the diaries and books you brought me in 1965. There were CDs as well ... had years waiting for those to work!"

"What did you do for your research work then, if it wasn't in time travel?" I asked, picking up the axe, and squaring up to the controls in the cubicle.

"Oh, I specialised in climate change," he said with a giggle.

"Climate change?"

"Oh just say that I am sucker for things that people refuse to believe in!"

I held the axe low, breathed in and then flexed my muscles ready to swing. A thought occurred to me.

"You know, back in my first timeline, I was running off, not doing my research, complaining, not telling you about what I was doing and generally messing you around ... but you still knew that I would come back to 1965 because you had met me there already."

"Well," he said, "somehow I must have believed that you would come good in the end and trusted you to survive all your blunders. I am told that that is what being a parent is like."

I let the axe sway in my grip as I thought about the world that no longer existed, the world that I had known.

"What about me? Do you even know me in this timeline? I mean, without your time travel research, there would be no reason for me to study in Cardiff and ..."

Leeds was laughing now, "This time when I interviewed you, you told me that you didn't want to study too far from home. You're a PhD student here researching climate change."

"Really? And what am I like to supervise?"

"I'm not your supervisor but Braithwaite assures me that you are annoying, impetuous, frustrating, you don't listen and you don't take things seriously."

"Wow, I'm really different, aren't I?"

"No self-reflection either."

I drew the axe back but then wobbled slightly. Leeds reached out an arm towards me but I regained my balance.

"There's a chair behind you," he said kindly, "take a moment, we've got time."

As I had prepared to swing the axe, I had felt the time lag surge into me as my initial euphoria dissipated. Now the memories of this timeline start to wash into me. They would sit in my mind opposite the ones from all the other timelines I had lived in. No wonder each journey had only made me more confused and older than my years.

It felt like I was underwater and heading towards the surface, the light of the new memories visible in the distance, waiting to become clearer when I surfaced. I looked at Leeds with surprise and confusion.

"You ... we ... I was at the Millennium Centre with you. We went to see 'War Horse' together, the puppetry! You and ... oh my goodness, there's a Mrs Leeds!"

"There was," he corrected me gently, "sadly no more."

"I'm sorry. But, we were ... friends?"

Leeds sighed and looked around the room behind me as he spoke, "When I met you in '65 you seemed ... sad and isolated. You know what I realised, Demi. People with an extraordinary or an unusual talent, they're always on their own. And we ... lonely people, we have to stick together. So yes, within the limits of academic professionalism of course ..."

My mind whirred with new images. Moving house, fixing the back gate, going to the Bay after pay day and that memory from the Millennium Centre slowly started to fill in all its senses - sight first, then sound, then smell, taste and ...

"When you were with us watching 'War Horse', what did your left hand feel like?" he asked.

I held my left hand as if it had its own memory rushing back into it. I knew it, I felt it - another hand holding mine! Warm, re-assuring, sharing the experience together, my world starting and ending with him and us, oh my world, I was so in love with him, so very present and warm and safe beside him!

"I have a boyfriend?" I asked, not really believing it.

"Not any more, I'm afraid," he said, "but you did. Mary and I were quite convinced you were going to marry, had you round for dinner a few times."

"I managed to screw that up as well, did I?"

"He had to go back to Dublin to study, I'm afraid. You're going to get those memories of how broken your heart was too, I'm so sorry about that. But you know that's the thing, isn't it? Once you know it's possible, you know it can happen again."

I was starting to cry, but Leeds had reminded me of everything I needed to know. I was happier in this new time line. I was more ... me, all the good and all the bad, all the pain, all the joy, all the happiness, all the misery, all the sorrow, all the triumph, all the failure ... all me.

"It's time," I said, picking up the axe and then letting out a teary cry of exhilarated joy as my first blow struck through the control panel.

Part 7

My audience were filing out of the hall and I returned the projector screen to the opening title, 'The World's First Female Time Traveller'. No-one would stay for questions when there was food available and, anyway, I knew that time travel was impossible in this timeline.

I walked to the back of the hall, where one figure was standing alone with a smirk on her face, clapping me slowly. It was my best friend-in-law and I had invited her specially.

"I don't think that your portrayal of me caught my best side," said Sarah with a smile.

"You did try to hit me," I countered.

"No," she said, shaking her head, "I'd never do that to the person who brought me to my wife."

With that, she gave me an unexpected hug and whispered 'well done', which could have been about the presentation or introducing her to Georgie, I was not sure which and did not feel like asking. Sarah was wearing the smart suit of a business delegate, her life very different to the one I had just described.

"'Sarah Evans' is a bloody hard name to find, you know. I thank your parents for putting 'Alvara' in the middle!"

Sarah laughed at that and added, "It was weird enough when you phoned me and implored me to get to some pub to meet an Australian woman who was just my type. Had I not been on the dating websites, I would have never been fooled. Still, I am glad that we were your last errand."

"Ah, but it was not me who you met, that was the 19 year old me who Georgie was visiting, who I knew would be there and would recognise her friend falling in love when she saw it."

Sarah shook her head again to show that she thought that I was talking nonsense, "Well, I am touched that even in your fiction, you're a good friend to us both."

"And how's my godson?" I asked to hide my embarrassment at the compliment.

"Duncan? Ooo, he's adorable. Starting to give us a bit of a let up with sleep and everything, but still great. You do know that Georgie's parents still say that she came to visit you and you turned their daughter into a lesbian?"

"It was sleeping with women that did that to the girl," I replied and then thought that I might have heard that said before but I could not remember where or whether anyone else would remember it.

Sarah was smiling though, "You've been a good friend to us, Demi. You know that, we both really value you. In your stories you sound like a bit ... don't take this the wrong way, a bit ..."

"There's no-one else quite like me," I suggested.

"That's one way of saying it!" she said, laughing again, indicating to me to follow her through the door into the lunch area, "We've always liked that spirit though - you just go for it. You make the most of things, you know. Anyway, I'm glad that all the time travel stuff is obviously fiction."

"Really?" I asked, intrigued as to what mistake she thought that she had seen in the presentation.

"You know the pregnancies, the ... the ones we lost. That ... no-one could put her friend through that and not want to change it. I would change it if I could."

Sarah's voice was breaking a little as she said this and it would have seemed wrong to point out that I had dealt with that dilemma in my presentation. No-one should be put in the position of being a God, deciding for other people what they experience.

In his own patient way, Professor Leeds had taught me that. His fretting while I travelled and his faith that I would come good in the end showed a far greater love than had he stopped me making mistakes.

Sarah touched my elbow and tried to bring me forwards into the room.

"Ah well, at least in your story I get to be the world's first female time traveller," she said with a chuckle.

"The second," I replied firmly, "the second."

"What about those books you said that you mentioned when we argued? You were about number five?"

"Fiction," I said, "I was real."

Sarah had already walked towards the buffet table though and was queuing for bread and cheese. I turned back to look at the empty conference room.

Some of the chairs still had bags and coats on them and there were bundles of scientific papers waiting to be picked up again. On the screen at the front of the hall, my first slide was still showing. "The World's First Female Time Traveller" it said.

"Alpha and Omega," I muttered to myself.

For some reason, I reached over to the light switches for the hall. I switched each of them off one by one until it was just me at the back of the room looking through the darkness at the screen, illuminated by the final light.

"I was the first, I am the first and I will be the first ... and the last," I said and then I switched off that final light.

I stared into the darkness of the empty hall and said to no-one in particular, "Not even the stars survive."

Printed in Great Britain
by Amazon

70555060R00051